Rina stood. "It's gett

He rose to his feet. "Yeah
you can give me the parts
long for me to fix."

The sink—that was right. He'd made her forget all about it...along with her troubles. She didn't open up like that with anyone.

Back at the café, after handing him the parts, she pulled the inventory for tomorrow's food prep.

A short time later, Scott knocked on the doorjamb of her office. "I'm all done. Do you want to take a look?"

She followed him to the ladies' room and tried out the faucet. The knob was back on. Water was flowing from where it should, and there were no leaks.

Rina faced him. "Thank you for taking care of this, and thank you for listening to me earlier."

"No problem." He picked up the toolbox from the floor. "And you won, by the way. I owe you ice cream."

"No. I owe you ice cream. You having to act as a decoy for Nash is a lot more intriguing than my situation."

"As a rule, I don't argue over ice cream, so it's a date."

Rina headed to the front of the café with Scott. A date? No, it wasn't a date, just an expression. They'd made a bet, she'd lost and was paying up by buying him ice cream. That was all.

Dear Reader,

Thank you for choosing *Her Sweet Temptation* as your new romance escape.

As the owner of Brewed Haven Cafe, Zafrina "Rina" Tillbridge makes the best pies in town while juggling the tasks of being the boss and keeping up with expectations. Stuntman Scott Halsey is used to taking risks and living life on his own. Their worlds literally collide, and their lives change in unexpected ways.

Moving on from the past, taking chances to discover new passions, letting go of perfection, embracing family despite their faults—Rina and Scott face these experiences in this book. The best part is they learn and grow together. And they have dessert along the way.

I'd love to hear from you. Visit me at www.ninacrespo.com, say hello and connect with me. Instagram, Facebook and my newsletter are three of my favorite places to connect with readers. I share about my books, upcoming appearances and a few of the dessert recipes I came across during my research for this story.

Rina and Scott are waiting for you. I hope you enjoy their journey to finding love and the rest of the Tillbridge Stables series!

Happy reading,

Nina

Her Sweet Temptation

NINA CRESPO

**HARLEQUIN®
SPECIAL
EDITION™**

ISBN-13: 978-1-335-89487-8

Her Sweet Temptation

Copyright © 2020 by Nina Crespo

Harlequin Enterprises ULC
22 Adelaide St. West, 40th Floor
Toronto, Ontario M5H 4E3, Canada
www.Harlequin.com

Printed in U.S.A.

Nina Crespo lives in Florida, where she indulges in her favorite passions—the beach, a good glass of wine, date night with her own real-life hero and dancing. Her lifelong addiction to romance began in her teens while on a "borrowing spree" in her older sister's bedroom, where she discovered her first romance novel. Let Nina's sensual contemporary stories feed your own addiction for love, romance and happily-ever-after. Visit her at ninacrespo.com.

Books by Nina Crespo

Harlequin Special Edition

Tillbridge Stables

The Cowboy's Claim
Her Sweet Temptation

Visit the Author Profile page
at Harlequin.com for more titles.

Chapter One

Zafrina Tillbridge drove over one of the many bumps on the vacant tree-lined road. As the bronze SUV shimmied and bounced, an image sprang up in her mind of the perfectly flaky crusts on the apple, peach and blueberry pies stowed in the rear of the vehicle crumbling to bits. Taking the two-lane short-cut that morning as a faster way to Tillbridge Horse Stable and Guesthouse was the worst idea of her entire week. And it was just Monday.

A couple of months ago, the location scouts for the sci-fi Western movie, *Shadow Valley*, that was currently being filmed at Tillbridge had stopped by Brewed Haven, the cafe she owned in Bolan, and fallen in love with her pies. The film's production company had offered her a month-to-month catering contract, and she'd agreed to provide desserts once a week during lunch for the cast and crew of the film.

Zafrina hit another dip in the road and her inner perfectionist wailed. *This can't be happening.* Her first delivery for the contract, and instead of masterpieces, she was potentially delivering a mess.

The car system's ringtone came through the speakers and she glanced at the screen. It was her best friend, Philippa, the chef of Pasture Lane Restaurant and the manager of the guesthouse at Tillbridge. The restaurant was providing a special lunch for the cast and crew to celebrate the kickoff week for the filming of the movie. She was supposed to meet Philippa where they were setting up to serve the food at noon.

She clicked the answer button on her steering wheel. "Hi, Philippa."

"Hey, wh— are—?" The rest of what Philippa said was even more distorted by interference.

"What did you say? You're not coming in clearly."

More garbled words came through then the line went dead.

It had sounded like Philippa was asking, "Where are you?" or maybe it was, "Why aren't you here yet?" Either question wasn't a good one. The buffet was probably set and ready to go…minus her desserts.

Finally, Zafrina reached the intersection to the empty main road. Just a couple of more miles and she'd arrive at the stable.

A red truck came out of nowhere and blew past from the left.

Zafrina gripped the steering wheel and jammed her foot on the brake. Hot-and-cold prickles of alarm and relief rained over her, and the jeans and lemon yellow T-shirt she wore suddenly became too warm and not warm enough at the same time.

An elusive memory of a curved road she couldn't place started to slip into her thoughts. *No.* The car was gone, and she was okay. She needed to get to Tillbridge. Taking in a long, slow breath and releasing an even longer exhale, she eased down on the accelerator and turned right.

Farther down the road, she passed by a gently sloping fenced-in pasture, and she opened the driver-side window breathing in the earthy scents of rich earth and lush green grass warmed by the sun, and horses. Echoes of the past filled with happiness, perseverance, and triumph filled her mind. Even though she didn't live on the property anymore, Tillbridge would always be home.

Uniformed guards controlled access to the paved parking lot behind the large horse stable.

Still not used to the increased security on the property because of the film production, Rina dug through the center console for her VIP badge. After parking in one of the few vacant spaces, she grabbed her things from the front passenger seat and got out. As she put on the purple apron printed with the cafe's name and logo of hearts winding up like steam from a coffee cup, a summer breeze blew through her black braids secured by a yellow band.

Chestnut, sable and gray horses roamed around the paddock on the far right adjoining the sandstone-colored stable that had a navy roof and trim.

The lunch buffet was supposed to be set up near the picnic tables in the outdoor seating area yards down from the building. Where were the white tents and the lime-green van from Pasture Lane?

She called Philippa who answered on the second ring. "Hey, Rina." Like most of Zafrina's friends and family, Philippa used the shortened version of her name.

"Where are you?"

"And hello to you too," Philippa replied. A faint southern lilt wove through her words.

"Sorry." Rina closed her eyes a moment. "I'm having a crazy day. Aren't we supposed to set up in the picnic area by the stables?"

"There was a change of plans and they're running late. That's why I was calling you earlier. When I couldn't get through, I sent you a text."

Messages chimed in and Rina glanced at the notifications on her phone. One text was from Philippa about the changes. The other was from Darby, who was working a split shift at the cafe, leaving for the afternoon and returning later that evening:

Right sink in the ladies' room starting to drip. Need more bulbs—the light in the storeroom is flickering again. A guy stopped by and filled out an application. It's on your desk.

Rina added buying florescent bulbs and finding a plumber to her growing mental to-do list. She'd look over the application when she returned.

Just over a week ago, she'd unexpectedly lost one of her key employees who handled maintenance at the cafe and made the deliveries. Now she and her staff were struggling to take up the slack. If the person who'd stopped by had the right qualifications to fill the position, she'd set up an interview with him as soon as possible.

"Hellooo," Philippa called out over the phone. "Are you still there?"

"Yes. I was glancing over the messages I missed. I'm just getting them. I came the back way. My cell reception dropped out."

"You drove here on that pothole-infested road? Why?"

Rina muzzled her excuse. She'd wanted to save time, but in retrospect, her reasoning had been more than just a little faulty. "It's a long story. I'll tell you when I see you. Where are we setting up now?"

"Halfway across the field past the new barn."

Rina looked behind her, spotting the food van and two white tents in the distance. "Be there in a sec."

"Oh and—"

Rina hung up prematurely. *Oops*. But in a few

minutes, Philippa could tell her what she'd started to say.

At the back of the SUV, Rina slipped the phone in her front apron pocket and opened the rear door. Had the pies survived? She slid one of the four sheet pans with semiclear lids from the plastic travel container and peeked inside. A breath of relief whooshed out. But now wasn't the time to celebrate. She still had to get the pies where they belonged.

Rina lifted the sheet pan to her shoulder, closed the rear door, and started across the mown pasture. She'd ask one of Philippa's staff to get the rest of the desserts.

As she trekked to the catering area yards ahead, she saw Philippa dressed in beige chef's gear and wearing her signature lime-green bandana as a headband over her dark dreadlocks. She was placing serving utensils on a long empty buffet table under the first tent while her staff was checking over the setup of tables and foldable chairs in the other tents nearby.

In front of Rina to the right, orange cones were stationed a short distance from the open entrance of the new distressed-wood barn that had been built for the film. Funny, it almost felt as if the small barn had always been there. Maybe because years ago there used to be one on the property. The stable had been much smaller, and there hadn't been a guesthouse, just a large family home where she lived with her parents, Mathew and Cherie, her sister, Zurie, her cousin, Tristan, and his father, Jacob.

Rina couldn't stop a smile as she thought of summers at Tillbridge back then. As the oldest by more than five years, a teenaged Zurie had been responsible for looking after her and Tristan during the day while their parents worked, although Tristan had believed his role was being their protector. While Zurie was taking care of the big-girl chores—making breakfast and lunch for the three of them and checking on the horses—she and Tristan would sneak off to the empty field to play ball, climb trees and play hide-and-seek.

Ready or not, here I come... The recollection of Tristan as a young boy calling out to her younger self filled her mind.

Philippa shouting pulled Rina back to the present, but she was too far away to hear what she was saying. Why was Philippa waving her arms above her head as if she was warning her off?

Chapter Two

Scott Halsey adjusted the black cowboy hat that was all but glued to his head then pulled on his dark leather fingerless gloves. As he altered his stance, the soles of his black boots scraped over the wide wood beam near the ceiling of the empty barn. The long black duster jacket, covering his dark vest and pants and the prop pistol in the holster strapped around his waist, sat hot and heavy on his shoulders.

Losing the coat would make him a lot cooler, but even though they were just rehearsing the stunt for the movie, they needed to duplicate conditions for the filming of the scene, and that included knowing how the costume would affect movement. But a barn steadily heating up from the sun was nothing compared to other situations he'd endured. During his career as a stuntman, he'd been submerged in freezing water, baked in the desert and set on fire from head to toe.

As he reached for the cord in front of him secured to a metal girder above his head, tingles of anticipation danced up and down his spine. He harnessed the familiar feeling into an intense focus that became sharper and narrower as he breathed.

The stunt he was practicing rated low on the danger spectrum. In fact, it reminded him of the rope swing he and his sister played on during summer vacations when they were kids. The only difference, he wasn't flying as high as he could on a dare and dropping into a lake. He was swinging over the floor of the barn, and if he aimed properly, which he would, once he let go of the rope he'd land just outside. From that point, it was an easy drop and roll to his knee before unholstering the empty pistol and aiming at the nonexistent bad guys.

He glanced down at the balding light-haired stunt coordinator, Kyle, and the two college-aged interns wearing jeans and black T-shirts with the name of the movie on the front and CREW on the back. "I'm ready."

Kyle motioned for the two guys to go outside then gave Scott a thumbs-up.

Scott's heart rate kicked up a tad as he tightened his hold on the cord. He leaped off the beam and swung down. As he soared through the air, his senses heightened and his vision focused on the threshold of the open barn doors. But instead of a clear path in front of him, a woman carrying a tray was walking past.

As she glanced his way, she froze. Shock came over her face and her mouth formed an O.

Decisions synced in his mind. He dropped short of his mark on the shock-absorbing pad, executed a tighter roll than planned, and sprang to his feet.

As he wrapped an arm around the flabbergasted woman's slender waist, she released a sound between a scream and a squeak. He braced his other hand under the tray with hers, catching it before it slipped to the ground.

Her eyes, a spectrum of hues from deep gold to sepia, met his. She breathed unsteadily and a glow tinged her smooth dark brown cheeks. Taking hold of the tray, she slipped from his grasp. "Are you out of your mind? What are you doing?"

He didn't mean to chuckle, but the exasperated expression on her pretty face was more cute than threatening. Scott tipped his hat and gave his best charming fake Western drawl. "My job, ma'am."

"So you get paid to crash into people?"

"On occasion, but I just performed some of my greatest work."

She gave him a puzzled look. "What?"

"I saved two out of two. You and these." He glanced down to the sheet pan clutched in her hands. The lid was halfway off...and what looked to be two pies were smooshed against the side of it. "Damn.

I thought I nailed it. I'm sorry. Here, let me carry that for you."

"No. You've done enough already." Her tone was soft but firm as she turned slightly away from him putting the sheet pan out of reach. "Move please."

He stepped aside and she walked away. Again.

He'd noticed her yesterday morning near the stable where the restaurant food van was parked. Kyle had asked him to meet him there for breakfast so they could talk about the rigging for the barn stunt.

She'd been talking to Tristan, the stable manager and one of the owners of Tillbridge. He'd assumed they were related because she resembled the tall man with low-cut dark hair, and it was easy to see that they shared a close bond. Every time she'd laughed, she'd radiated happiness, and he'd had to force himself not to stare at her. During his meeting with Kyle, his mind had kept wandering back to her, wondering who she was. By the time they'd finished, she was gone.

Feet away, Kyle's face was red with frustration as he bellowed at the interns. "What the heck happened? You were supposed to make sure no one wandered through the area."

Scott took off his hat. He still didn't know her name. Would a second apology give him a chance to find out who she was? Maybe he could use it as an excuse to start a conversation with her.

Kyle intersected his path, stopping him from following her. "Things looked great up until the landing, but good job on the recovery. That could have been a real disaster. Is she okay?"

Scott reluctantly took his gaze away from her and focused on Kyle. "I think so." He released a wry laugh. "But she's not happy. I'm lucky she didn't bite my head off."

"The quick thinking you just did is the prime reason I don't want Nash doing his own stunts. The ability to adjust like that at the last minute is all about instinct and experience. He just won't accept that he's not there yet."

"You're still getting pressure from him?"

"Yeah. Now that he's gone through some stunt training, he thinks he's a professional. And it doesn't help that he's the lead actor for this movie, but as easy as this stunt looks to Nash, if I let him do it and he gets hurt, the director, the insurance company and the rest of the film backers will have my ass. That's why this rehearsal is off the grid with just the four of us. I didn't want him butting in about what he thinks he can do. As far as I'm concerned, if Nash hasn't rehearsed it, he won't do it. Period."

Scott understood Kyle's pain. There were actors that wouldn't risk getting a scratch, and then there were those like Nash Moreland who believed doing their own stunts brought authenticity to their action scenes or, sometimes, it was about the bragging rights to impress their fans.

Scott tipped his head toward the barn. "If we rig

a harness to the beam, I'm ninety-five percent sure he can do this one without a problem."

Kyle released a gruff chuckle. "Harness or not, I need ninety-nine point nine percent certainty before I make that decision. Right now, my main concern is you nailing this without any problems. We need to get this done before lunch starts and the cast and crew show up. You ready to try it again, this time without interference?"

"Let's do it." As Scott lifted his hand to wipe sweat from his brow, a streak of what looked to be fruit filling and pie crust on the back of his fingers stopped him. He licked over it and sweetness perked up his taste buds.

Blueberries. Not bad. Scott's gaze strayed over to the woman he had yet to meet standing under the tent. Not bad at all.

Chapter Three

"Are you okay?" Philippa took the peach and apple pies from the sheet pan Rina was holding and arranged them on the buffet table.

"Yes. But what am I going to do with these?" Rina tipped her head toward the two ruined blueberry pies.

"Just stick a spoon in them instead of a spatula. There's space for them right here." Philippa put them next to the other pies.

"But they look terrible. They're supposed to be round not smashed."

"Relax, Ms. Patty Perfect." Humor shown in Philippa's coppery-brown eyes bringing out the youthful glow in her light brown face that had a smattering of freckles. "They're still good. Trust me. If this past weekend is an indication of how this crowd eats, the only thing left will be crumbs."

"They're lucky to have pies at all." Rina couldn't stop herself from glancing toward the guy who'd practically mowed her over and ruined her desserts. He was talking with the balding middle-aged man who'd come out of the barn after their run-in. Philippa had said they were rehearsing a stunt for the movie.

Philippa nudged her. "Stop glaring at the poor guy. I tried to warn you the area was blocked off. How did you miss the big orange cones?"

"I was distracted."

"By what?"

She and Philippa had both been so busy lately they hadn't had a moment to catch up. "Dennis handed in his resignation a little over a week ago."

Philippa turned towards her. "Dennis, the fixer of all things, resigned? You're joking."

That had been her response when the sixty-two-year-old who'd been with her from the beginning, and had served as the maintenance man for the bakery that had resided in the space before the cafe, had told her that he was leaving. "No, it's not a joke. He said he needed an adventure."

"An adventure? What exactly is he planning to do for excitement in Bolan?"

"That's the even bigger surprise. He's not staying in town. He bought a one-way ticket to Alaska.

He even turned his house into an Airbnb and found someone to manage things while he's gone."

"Wow." Philippa shook her head. "I wonder what got into him? I hope he knows what he's doing."

"I do, too."

Eight years ago, when she was nineteen, she'd left town with her then boyfriend, Xavier, looking for the same thing. But instead of adventure, she'd encountered disappointment and heartache instead. Hopefully Dennis wouldn't experience the same.

Rina picked up a serving spoon from the table and stuck it in one of the blueberry pies. "Until I can find someone to replace him, the staff and I are taking care of deliveries and all of the tasks he used to do, but repairs are starting to pile up, and I'm behind in making the desserts for tomorrow's tasting with the buyer from Gwen's Garden."

The natural foods market chain was interested in offering her a wholesaler's contract to provide pies for their local stores. Weeks ago when the opportunity popped up, she'd been thrilled. But almost overnight, a windfall of opportunities had suddenly turned into an avalanche of worries. How was she supposed to get it all done?

Philippa patted her arm. "I know how much you counted on him. No wonder you're stressed. I can check in with some of my people and see if they're interested in working for you on their days off or after their shifts. You could also talk to Tristan about sending a maintenance worker from here to help out with repairs."

"No, I don't want to overwork your staff. You need them for all the catering you're doing for this contract, and I don't want to bother Tristan either. He has his hands full trying to coordinate Tillbridge's work schedule with the filming of the movie."

Philippa arched her brow. "From the smile on his face these days, he's handling it just fine."

"I'm sure we have Chloe to thank for that."

"Definitely."

A few short months ago, Chloe Daniels, an actress, had come to Tillbridge to research life at a horse stable for an audition. They'd fallen for each other. She'd since won the part in *Shadow Valley*, and now Chloe and Tristan were both excited about spending more time together while she worked on the film.

"If you don't want to bother Tristan, there is another way." From the look in Philippa's eyes, Rina already knew what she was going to say.

"Ask Zurie instead of Tristan for help? That's a huge nope. First, I'd get the judgy look, then I'd get a lecture from her on what I should have done to prevent Dennis from leaving and after that, she'd try to micromanage whoever she sent over to *my* cafe to help out. It's not worth the headache."

Philippa held her hands up in surrender. "It was just a suggestion. She is the co-manager of the entire operation along with Tristan."

It wasn't a bad idea, but these days, Rina didn't have energy for the smile, ignore, deflect game she usually played with Zurie whenever she talked to her. "Someone called the cafe today looking for a job. They could work out, and who knows, Dennis could change his mind and come back."

"Maybe."

Rina followed Philippa's gaze that had shifted to the two men in front of the barn. "I didn't know middle-aged guys were your thing. Don't be shy. Prance on over there and say hello to him."

"I don't prance. I walk gracefully. And if I were interested in saying hello to anyone, it would be the guy that ran into you. He's Nash Moreland's stunt double, and in my opinion, he's a lot better looking than Nash."

Thirtyish, dirty blond hair on the longish side, a five o'clock shadow covering his angled jawline, hazel green eyes with more than a hint of mischief to match his easy smile. It did all fit together for an appealing package. "He's okay."

"Just okay? You wouldn't say that if you saw him without the jacket. He had it off earlier when he came over here to ask for some water. Girl…" Philippa fanned her face. "After seeing him up close, I needed water to cool off. Too bad this film isn't about lifeguards."

Rina's own imagination wandered into Philippa's daydream territory, rewinding to when he'd effortlessly held her up while keeping the tray of pies from falling to the ground. Then it morphed into him without the jacket, wrapping his strong arms around her while she leaned into his solid, muscular chest. Heat started to flush into her cheeks, and she swept the image aside. Now wasn't the time for fantasies.

"Everyone will be here soon. Shouldn't you bring out the rest of the food?"

"Probably." Even though the two men had gone back inside the barn, Philippa still stared in that direction. "He looked intense when he came over here. I wonder what he's like when he's not working?"

The teasing, sexy, oh-so-confidant smile he'd flashed after "saving the pies" came into Rina's mind.

Nash Moreland's double sailed out of the barn, and in one fluid movement, he rolled to a crouching position with the prop pistol in his hand.

The way he performed that stunt so easily and mindlessly told Rina all she needed to know. Just like Xavier, he viewed himself as invincible.

Chapter Four

Scott parallel parked the red two-door compact near the sidewalk in downtown Bolan. Even though it was almost eight thirty at night, people still mingled along Main Street.

The small town was on trend with other revitalized provincial paradises he'd come across during his travels. They even had the requisite quaint sign on the way in: Welcome to Bolan. Friends and Smiles for Miles Live Here.

In the center of the area, a town square with neatly clipped grass and flowering bushes featured a large stone water fountain surrounded by park benches. Old-fashioned-styled streetlamps illuminated a path through the square. They also lined the sidewalks on either side of him in front of small businesses including an ice cream parlor, a floral shop, a bookstore, a dress boutique, a wine bar and the Brewed Haven Cafe across the street on the corner. Unlike the other businesses that were linked together in strip mall fashion, the two-story light-colored brick cafe with large storefront windows stood on its own.

Rina Tillbridge. He'd finally found out her name from one of the staff at Pasture Lane Restaurant. They'd also told him she owned the cafe.

Grateful to stretch his legs that were tight from a long day of rehearsing stunts then riding in the small car, Scott grabbed his phone from the cup holder in the middle console between the seats and got out.

He usually drove his SUV or rode his Harley to a job whenever he could, but Kyle had needed him in Maryland sooner than later. The stuntman originally hired to double for Nash Moreland had hurt himself rock climbing right before he was supposed to show up for the filming of *Shadow Valley*. With Scott having doubled for Nash in the past, he'd been called to replace the injured stuntman. Home early in Los Angeles from working on an independent film production in Hawaii, he'd been looking forward to a couple of weeks of downtime, but Kyle had given him his first movie job and recommended him to several other stunt coordinators. After all Kyle had done for his career, he couldn't turn him down.

Lights in the cafe illuminated the storefront window. The scene of people sitting at wood tables with single-flower centerpieces and in the light purple

booths lined along the wall, enjoying food, caffein-
ated drinks and conversation, drew more than a few
pedestrians inside.

The bright decor reminded him of Rina Tillbridge's vibrant laughter. He would have preferred
hearing her laugh instead of ticking her off that
morning.

So you get paid to crash into people?

*On occasion, but I just performed one of my
greatest stunts. I saved two out of two.*

Yeah, he'd actually thrown out that line with a
fake drawl and a smile, expecting her to smile back
at him. But from the look on her face, he'd come off
as cocky instead. By the time he and Kyle had finished running through the stunt two more times,
she was leaving.

He'd spotted her in the distance trekking across
the pasture to the parking lot. The hitch in her step
had probably been imperceptible to everyone else,
but he'd covered up enough aches and pains in his
time to notice. Had he caused it? He'd been so proud
of himself for making the correction in his landing
he hadn't thought to ask if she was okay.

The breeze from passing cars ruffled his slate gray
pullover. Scott tucked the keys in the front pocket of
his jeans. As he crossed the street to Brewed Haven,
his phone rang and he checked the screen. It was his
younger sister. If Wendy was calling him about what
he thought she was, it wouldn't be a short conversation. Scott tapped Ignore and walked into the cafe.

Waitstaff in purple T-shirts with the cafe's yellow logo served customers in the dining area to his right. The two baristas at a curved station in front of him were just as busy preparing coffees and serving up desserts from the glass showcase below the service counter.

Some of the customers just grabbing coffees or desserts migrated to an alcove on the left. Round tables along with beige couches with purple throw pillows tucked into spaces under the three side windows filled the smaller space.

Was Rina still there? According to the sign on the door, they closed in thirty minutes. Maybe she'd already gone home for the night.

Scott took a seat in a high-backed stool at the long dining counter that branched off from the coffee service area into the main dining space. The pleasing scents of succulent food wafted over him and his mouth watered. He'd had dinner with members of the crew earlier that evening, but that was hours ago. He could still eat. He perused the plastic-covered menu featuring burgers, sandwiches, various entrées and desserts.

A short time later a curvy, twenty-something brunette with a short hi-low bob and lightly tanned skin came over to him. "Welcome to Brewed Haven. My name is Darby. Can I get you coffee or another beverage?"

"Iced tea would be great. Is Rina Tillbridge still

here? I know it's late, but if she has a minute, I'd really like to speak with her."

Recognition came into her blue eyes seeming to imply she knew who he was. Maybe she'd seen him with the crew at Tillbridge? Many of the locals were patronizing the restaurant in the guesthouse where he was staying, hoping to run into Nash.

"Oh right, you're here to see Rina." Skepticism filled her face. "I don't know, maybe if you'd come by earlier, but now…"

"If she's busy, I can wait." Two plates piled high with meatloaf, mashed potatoes and what looked to be fresh green beans that a server was delivering to customers at a nearby table snagged Scott's attention. "And if the kitchen hasn't closed yet, I'd like to order the special."

Darby's brows raised as she gave him a strange look. "One meatloaf special. Got it."

A server flagged Darby down on the other side of the room. She rushed away before he could give her his name.

Rina added butter to the bowl in the mixer sitting on the metal prep counter along the wall in the kitchen. After adjusting the attachment, she turned the mixer on. As it whirred away, she leaned a bit on the counter, easing some of the weight from her right leg. Her knee ached a little more than usual from stomping on the brake that morning when the truck had sped out of nowhere on the main road.

When she'd gotten back from Tillbridge, she'd considered taking a short break upstairs in her apartment, but she had too much to do, and she'd also arranged an interview right before dinner service with the guy who'd inquired about the job. He had an impressive background having worked as a handyman and also as a kitchen helper at a hotel restaurant. He'd called back to say he couldn't make it until later. They'd rescheduled to meet thirty minutes ago, but he'd still failed to show up.

The pies she'd made for tomorrow's tasting with Gwen's Garden, now cooling on a rack farther down the counter, wouldn't fall in the failure category. Their recipes had been passed down through her family on her mother's side, in some cases for multiple generations. As a little girl, her mother had taught her how to correctly measure out the ingredients and balance the flavors of salty, tart and sweet.

Baking the pies brought her close to the comfort she used to experience when she'd gotten on her horse and settled into her favorite English saddle. Peace, accomplishment, the feeling of freedom as she and her horse soared over fences in the arena. Wistfulness pinged inside of Rina. But her competition days were long over. Brewed Haven was the priority now.

In the middle of the steel blue floored space with industrial stainless steel appliances, cooks worked in tandem preparing food.

The dark-haired head cook, Ben, plated the servers' orders and set them up with service tickets in a large pass-through window opening to an adjoining corridor.

On the far side of the kitchen, more staff ran dirty dishes through the dish machine.

Luckily, service was running smoothly, and she'd been able to concentrate on baking pies and trying out a new dessert recipe that had caught her eye. She'd come across it in a magazine at her dentist's office the other week. Maybe she'd just been hungry at the time, but she'd torn out the page, stuck it in her bag and baked the pear bars that same day upstairs in her apartment.

They'd turned out okay, but something had prompted her to try the recipe again today after preparing the pies for the tasting. This time she was adding a little more cinnamon and a dash of ginger to the pears and the topping. Once they were done, she'd give them to the staff as a treat.

As she turned off the mixer, Darby, the cafe's dining supervisor, came over to her. "The guy who called about the job finally showed up."

"He did?" Rina scraped the contents for the dough out of the bowl onto a small metal sheet pan. "Did he mention why he's late?"

"No. But he did say he realized it was late. After that, he ordered the meatloaf special."

"Food is his first priority? Un-be-lievable." Rina set the bowl aside. "I guess he doesn't really want the job." All of her people were reliable. She wouldn't risk hiring someone who wasn't.

"What do you want me to tell him?"

"Nothing. Let him enjoy his meatloaf. I'll be out there to talk to him in a minute."

Darby's sigh came with a slightly glum expression. "Too bad he missed his chance. He's really cute and he has strong-looking hands."

Rina laughed. "We don't need someone who's nice to look at. We need someone who's dependable."

"I know." Mischief glimmered in Darby's eyes. "But having this guy around sure would have made things interesting."

Darby left to grab the guy's meatloaf.

Rina rolled out the dough then spread it into the corners of the pan. He had strong hands? A chuckle escaped. That was interesting.

Since the filming had started at Tillbridge, a lot of the town's available women, including Darby, had their eye out for new guys to meet. Dating in a small town was difficult. The pickings beyond people you already knew were so slim any new person that showed up, reliable or not, became a tempting possibility.

The image of the stuntman floated into her mind. Like Philippa had pointed out, he *was* cute. Had he been flirting with her when he'd thrown out that lame two-out-of-two line? The possibility of that being the case reluctantly brought a smile. But she didn't need a guy connected to drama, pretend or otherwise, in her life. Unfortunately, that seemed to be what mostly existed in the wilds of dating.

A few months ago, after one glass of wine too many, she'd let Philippa darc her into creating a profile on a dating site. One of the guys she'd connected with had seemed decent. Several get-to-know-you texts and phone calls later, she finally agreed to meet him for dinner. But the night had gone downhill fast once his ex-fiancée walked into the place with her new boyfriend. Afterward, all she could think about was how much effort she'd put into being there. Hair and nail appointments. Shopping for a new dress. Driving an hour away to Baltimore. Wasted time and effort that should have been put into, not taken away from, Brewed Haven. After that epiphany, she hadn't dated anyone since.

Rina took her time spooning the pear filling over the dough then topped the fruit with a mix of sugar and spices. After she popped the pan in one of the convection ovens in the middle of the kitchen, she set the timer on the Fitbit wrapped around her wrist. The guy who'd shown up late for his interview should have been at least halfway through with his meal by now.

On the way out of the kitchen, she called to Ben who was still at the service window. "How's it going?"

Lean and studious-looking in a pair of dark-rimmed glasses, he gave her a thumbs-up and went back to work.

She strolled into the wide corridor.

Farther down, servers set up their trays with drinks at the beverage station across from the pass-through window in the kitchen.

Rina went the opposite direction past the outer door to her office. A few feet ahead on the right, a wide archway led into the dining area that was emptying out as the cafe neared closing time.

Darby rang out customers at the register at the coffee service station. She spotted Rina and surreptitiously pointed to a lone blond guy sitting at the dining counter.

Rina couldn't see his entire face but his profile was familiar. No, it couldn't be…

He glanced her direction, and her steps faltered. It *was* him.

Shrieks came from the side hallway across the dining area, and Rina hurried that direction.

A young brunette walked out of the ladies' room on the left holding a little girl's hand.

Water dripped from the woman's face and the bangs of her shoulder-length hair. The front of her blue shirt was also soaked and water spots dotted the front of her jeans. Her Mini-Me's blue dress wasn't as wet but huge tears rolled down her rounded pale cheeks.

"Are you alright?" Rina asked.

The woman swiped hair from her eyes. "We're not hurt, just wet."

Water spattering on the bathroom tiles echoed through the closed door.

"I'm so sorry." Rina called to a server, "Grab some towels please." Shame heated her face. She didn't think the dripping sink was that urgent. What happened?

Darby instead of the server brought over a few of the clean side towels they used in the kitchen. They were small but sufficient enough for the woman to pat her and her little girl's face and arms dry.

Water was already seeping past the door into the hallway.

Rina took over towel duty freeing Darby to take care of the growing flood. "I have T-shirts that you can change into. And of course, your meal is on the house."

Irritation filled the woman's face, and she held up her hand as if planning to refuse the offer.

"Please." Rina looked directly into the woman's eyes. "I feel terrible this happened to you. Wouldn't dry T-shirts be more comfortable than wet clothes?"

"Well…" The woman glanced at her daughter. "It probably *would* be best for Evie to have on something dry for the ride home."

A little over twenty minutes later, a five-year-old Evie and her mom walked through the now-empty cafe. Both wore fresh-from-the-package Brewed Haven T-shirts.

Rina went with them to the door. "Again, I'm so sorry for the inconvenience."

"Well, I guess accidents do happen." Evie's mom looked down at her daughter. "I think getting sprayed with cold water was more of a shock than anything, right pumpkin?"

"Um-hmm." Evie agreed as she shoved a double chocolate chip cookie into her mouth with one hand while clutching a bag with more of the cookies that Rina had given them in the other.

As Evie and her mom walked to their car, Rina locked the door behind them and sagged against it. Her cheeks hurt from maintaining the smiles-for-miles Bolan attitude while hiding her embarrassment.

She shouldn't have ignored the issue with the faucet. Evie's mom said the cold water knob had popped off when she'd turned it and water had gushed into the air. How had a slow drip ended up turning into a geyser so fast?

Untimely repairs, that's what you can expect with old buildings…

The designer she'd hired five years ago when she'd renovated the space had pointed that out to her several times. And so had Zurie. She'd been the most vocal about not buying an older building. But it had good bones, and the original pedestal sinks in the bathrooms had character. The place had just needed some love, and Rina had poured hers into it along with a nice amount of cash. She had no regrets about doing it. And for years, Dennis's prior knowledge of the building's quirks and repair needs had kept things in order.

Weariness made her shoulders heavy. She just wanted to go upstairs and rest, but a long soak in her claw-foot tub would have to wait.

The sound of water being squeezed into a plastic bucket came from the side hallway. Seconds later, Darby rolled a cleaning bucket on wheels with a mop inside of it into the dining area.

Rina pushed away from the door and met her. "Thanks for staying behind to mop up. I'll call a plumber first thing in the morning."

"You may not have to. The handyman who showed up late for his interview is taking a look."

Was Darby referring to the Destroyer of Pies who broke things for a living? "You mean the guy waiting for me at the counter? He's not a handyman."

"He sure acted like one." Darby gave a pleased smiled. "He jumped right in and turned off the water valve under the sink then asked for tools to fix the faucet. He seems to know what he's doing. I brought him Dennis's toolbox."

"You what?"

Chapter Five

Rina rushed to the ladies' room and stopped in the doorway.

The Destroyer of Pies was crouched over the gray metal toolbox on the floor with a hammer in his hand.

Panic leaped inside of her. "Don't!"

He looked at her and his brows drew together with a puzzled look. "Don't what?"

"Don't break my sink."

"It's already broken. My plan is to fix it." He set the hammer aside on the floor next to his phone, took a metal wrench from the box and stood.

His beige Timberlands had damp spots on them. Wet spots also dotted the slightly faded jeans hugging his thighs and hips and his shirt stretching over his wide chest. The front of his hair was also damp and waves ran through it as if he'd recently raked it back from his face. He lifted the wrench and his bicep bulged. He held it like he knew what he was doing but looks could be deceiving.

Rina walked farther in. "I'm sorry, but I don't know your name."

"Scott."

He reached out his hand, and she slid her palm into his. The heat of his skin flowed into her like a current connecting them, holding her in place.

"I'm Rina." She took her hand from his but the warmth remained. "I appreciate you jumping in to help, Scott, but these sinks are—"

"Vintage. The real deal, not replicas." As he glanced around the ladies' room, an expression of appreciation came over his face. "Let me guess. The sinks inspired the design scheme."

Antique-style mirrors with decorative oval gold frames hung above the two white pedestal sinks that sat against pale lavender walls. Faux green plants in white pots were on corner shelves, and framed watercolor pictures of flowers hung on the back wall. Instead of metal-encased toilet cubicles, three floor-length dark-wood stalls provided style and privacy. The men's room also followed the same theme but had black-and-white color decor and touches that gave it a more masculine feel.

"You're two for two." The similarity to what he'd

said to her that afternoon drove her gaze to his. She hadn't meant to almost duplicate his words.

Sincerity deepened the color of his hazel-green eyes. "About this afternoon before lunch. I feel really bad about what happened. I'm sorry. I noticed you limping to the parking lot. Are you okay?"

Seven years ago, she'd survived one tragic accident, three surgeries and months of working her way mentally and physically back to health. The discomfort she dealt with now was nothing compared to what she'd gone through back then. But there was no need to open the door to that conversation. "I'm fine. And I accept your apology."

"Good." He pointed the wrench at the sink. "If you have spare parts for the faucet, I can fix this."

Just because he could recognize a real vintage sink from a replica didn't mean he had the skills to repair one. "I appreciate the offer, but I should probably find someone with experience."

"Experience." He chuckled. "Does shadowing my father at his plumbing company growing up plus working for him on kitchen, bath and pool design projects count?"

"Maybe."

"Here's the problem." Scott picked up the silver cross-shaped cold water knob that was lying in the sink. He flipped it over to the back side.

She leaned in and the invisible pull activated again drawing her into the pleasing woodsy scent with notes of tangerine, ginger and cardamom wafting from him. He smelled just as tempting as one of her desserts.

"Right here." He pointed. "See? It's cracked. When your customer turned it, the pressure of the water pushed it off. The good news is, the connection to the line in the sink is intact. You just need a new knob and seal. It's an easy fix."

Okay. His diagnosis of the problem and knowing how to repair it *was* a tad impressive. But there were plenty of good reasons for her to say no…and even better ones for her to say yes. He not only had plumbing experience, but he also hadn't told her she should get rid of the sinks because they were relics, and the biggest reason of all—she needed it done. Something inside of her said to trust him.

"Alright," Rina said. "I'm pretty sure we have the parts, but I won't be able to search for them until morning."

"I can come by tomorrow night. It might not be until eight or eight thirty."

"That's fine. I'll put a sign on the sink so people won't use it."

Silence lingered between them.

"Well…" They both said the word. He waited for her to speak first.

Rina pointed behind her at the open doorway. "I should finish closing down the kitchen and lock up."

"And I should let you do that, but first…" Scott stepped back and cool air magnified the loss of his closeness. He dropped the wrench and hammer inside the toolbox and picked up his phone. "I need your number."

Was he trying to ask her out on a date? Unexpected giddiness flushed warmth into her face. She really didn't need the distraction. Especially one that looked like him.

As he handed her his phone, a hint of a smile tilted up his mouth. "If I'm running later than expected, I'll call and let you know."

"Oh right." From the look on his face, he'd read her mind. As he watched her tap in the number, she messed up more than once. Of course he wasn't going to ask her out. Here she was thinking about how to let him down easy while all he was trying to do was make up for wrecking the pies.

Scott accepted his phone back from her and tapped the screen. "I called you so now you have mine, too."

Her phone was on the desk. She'd temporarily add him to her contacts later.

He picked up the toolbox and followed her to the dining area where Darby straightened chairs.

"Where do you want this?" He pointed to the toolbox.

"By the counter is okay."

As he put the box by one of the stools he glanced at the plate of pear bars on the counter in front of him. "Those smell good. What are they?"

"Pear bars. But they're not for sale. I'm still working on the recipe. I left those for the staff to try out."

"Is it okay if I taste one?"

"Yes, but like I said they're not perfected."

Scott picked up a bar. He took a bite and his brows shot up with a low deep hum of approval. "You're definitely on the right track. Mind if I take some for the road?"

Only the staff, family and close friends were allowed to sample her experiments, but the smile reaching into his eyes and highlighting the angles of his gorgeous face made her want to give him the entire plate. "Sure."

He took a large paper napkin from a stack on the counter next to the dessert and tucked three bars inside of it. "Thanks." Scott smiled as he sucked filling off his thumb. "I'll be back tomorrow to fix the sink."

As soon as he left, Darby came over to Rina with a confused look on her face. "I thought he wasn't the handyman?"

Chapter Six

A short time after leaving the cafe, Scott walked into his room at Tillbridge's guesthouse, his home for the next several weeks.

He wasn't high enough on the list to snag a private cottage on the property. Those were reserved for the director, Holland Ainsley, along with Nash Moreland and other main stars of the film. But as a thank you for helping him out, Kyle had pulled some strings and got him one of the few spaces available in the twenty-room guesthouse reserved for senior members of the crew.

Everyone else was staying at base camp—a group of trailers set up on the far side of the property for production, makeup, wardrobe, craft services as well as living quarters—or a chain motel down the road.

He set his keys and wallet on the dresser against the wall on the right, but the last dessert bar in the napkin beckoned. The delicious mix of spiced sweet pears and flaky pastry practically melted in his mouth. He'd been hooked on the bars after the first bite, and even more interested in getting to know Rina after talking to her. Working around celebrities, he ran into a lot of people who were superficial. Rina's smile was beautiful, but her laugh was even better. It was wholehearted and so carefree. There was also an appealing strength in her that was grounded and real.

Scott dropped down on the wood bench across from the dresser at the bottom of the queen-sized bed to take off his boots. Spending time with a woman had fallen low on the priority scale over the past few months. He just hadn't felt a strong enough connection with anyone to make the effort, but with Rina he'd felt something different. Not that he was looking for a deep relationship, just a low-key, let's-enjoy-ourselves arrangement, if she was interested.

When he'd asked for her number, from the way she'd looked at him, she'd probably thought he'd wanted to ask her out. And she'd planned to shoot him down. It didn't seem like she was still upset at him for running into her at the barn. Maybe she thought they didn't have anything in common. There were archived photos on his father's company website of projects he'd helped work on in the past. He could show her those and maybe that could lead to him inviting her out to hear more about what inspired her design ideas.

It was kind of funny that after all these years he was using plumbing and bath designs to get to know a pretty woman. But tinkering with the pedestal sink had actually brought back good memories of working with his dad growing up in New Jersey. How many years had passed since his father had taken him to that old Victorian home near Princeton? Twenty maybe? He'd been around eleven that summer and happy to spend time with his father who was still hands-on with his growing business.

Scott's phone rang on the dresser and he checked the screen. *Wendy.* If he didn't answer again, she'd keep calling. Her tenacity was one of the things that made her a great manager of their father's company.

As he answered the phone, he picked up the television remote on the dresser and turned on the flat screen above it on the wall. "Hey, boss lady."

"If I'm the boss, why are you dodging my calls?"

"I'm not dodging you. I was busy." Scott stretched out on the navy comforter on the bed and leaned against the headboard. "What's up?"

"You know exactly what's up. Dad's getting married in a few weeks. I know it's a long flight from Hawaii to Florida, but are you sure you can't fly in just for the weekend?"

Damn. Scott released a long exhale as he flipped through channels. He'd forgotten he hadn't told her or his father he was already back on the mainland. He could just not mention it.

An image came to his mind of when he was twelve and Wendy was nine. It was right before their parents' divorce. She'd nicked their right thumbs, pressed them together and made him swear they'd never lie to each other and always have each other's backs.

"I got back early from Hawaii," he said. "But now I'm working on a movie in Maryland, and my schedule is still tight."

"But you're even closer now. You can't miss his big day."

The "big day." He'd been through three of them with his father already since their parents' divorce, twice as his father's best man. "It's a Nash Moreland film so this is a major production. I have to be available when they need me. I already told Dad a few weeks ago I wouldn't be there and he understood. He'll get along fine without me this time. What's the rush with this marriage, anyway? They've only known each other a month?"

"He and Theresa have been together almost three months. And time together doesn't dictate whether a relationship is right or not. As strange as it sounds, I think this time he's gotten it right. Dad's in love."

Sure he was. That's what his father had said at the end of the weekend-long bachelor party in Vegas before the third wedding, and he'd believed him. But that trip down the aisle wasn't the charm. Neither was the fourth.

Scott tossed the remote on the bed. "I'm happy for him, but he said it wasn't going to be a big thing, just a small ceremony with a few close acquaintances on the beach."

"And family, which includes you. Are you sure you can't make it? It won't be the same for dad or me without you."

Scott rubbed his right index finger over his thumb where the scar remained. He loved Wendy and his dad, but pretending he was happy that his father was, once again, taking the vow of *until death do us part*… He just couldn't.

Chapter Seven

Rina adjusted the pies on the table at the cafe, ready for the 9:00 a.m. meeting with the representative from Gwen's Garden.

Customers carrying cardboard cups of coffee and large fluffy breakfast pastries glanced toward the side section where Rina stood. Noticing the two special event signs, they found a table up front.

A separate meeting space was something the cafe lacked. Six years ago, when she'd bought the corner building, turning the upstairs into conference rooms instead of an apartment had been a consideration, but she'd needed a place of her own—a true fresh start after the accident instead of continuing to reside at Tillbridge.

The door opened and Linda, the auburn-haired,

forty-something buyer for Gwen's Garden, came in with a younger dark-haired man who was immersed in his phone. Both gave off a corporate vibe in tailored business suits.

Linda had tried an apple pie from Brewed Haven at a friend's dinner party. She'd been impressed not only with the taste, but also how many of the party attendees, who didn't live near Bolan, had wished they could have access to the pies on a regular basis. Linda's enthusiasm when she'd contacted her along with her relaxed professional demeanor was what had encouraged Rina to explore the opportunity.

Rina wiped her palms down her apron, tamping down jitters as she walked over and greeted them.

"Hello." Linda shook her hand. "It's good to see you again." Just as she went to introduce her colleague, a call came in on his phone.

He offered a quick apologetic smile. "Hi, I'm Max. I have to take this. Excuse me a moment."

As he strolled back out of the cafe, Linda glanced his direction. "Max is our new assistant buyer. He's up to speed on what we discussed. Actually, he's already heard of Brewed Haven."

Was that a good sign?

Rina escorted Linda to the reserved tables, and a few minutes later Max joined them. While Linda tasted the pies and asked questions about ingredients and discussed what would be expected to fulfill the weekly orders, Max remained silent. He seemed more interested in drinking coffee than eating the desserts.

A little over an hour later, the tasting ended. "Thank you. We'll be in touch," Linda said.

Max gave a professional smile. "Nice meeting you."

After they left, as Rina and one of the servers cleared the tables where the tasting had taken place, she paused in picking up Max's plate. He'd barely sampled the peach pie that sat on it. It was one of the cafe's bestsellers. Did he not like peaches or pie in general? Linda had mentioned that he knew about Brewed Haven. Was he a fan of her desserts already? Maybe he'd already tasted them as a paying customer and didn't feel the need to do it now. If not, had she at least impressed Linda?

Anticipation kept her on edge the rest of the morning and afternoon. Every time her cell or the cafe's phone rang on her desk, she snatched it up, only to end up disappointed when it wasn't Linda. After oversalting the mashed potatoes for lunch and almost burning the gravy for the meatloaf entrée, she left the cooking to her staff and went to her office. Working on the next order with her main food distributer was a little harder to mess up. If she did, the ordering system on the website would beep at her.

Soon Rina was absorbed in the familiar task as she tapped on the computer keyboard sitting on her L-shaped black desk. A short stack of recipe books that belonged on the wall shelf behind her sat nearby.

To her left, a wide window provided a view of the kitchen. The sounds of clinking pots and dishes and sporadic conversation filtering in through the door beside it blended in as background noise she hardly noticed.

Her cell phone rang next to the books. Recognizing the number, she answered right away. "Hey, Philippa."

"Hi. How did the tasting go this morning?"

"Honestly—" Rina sank back in the black leather desk chair "—I'm not sure. The head buyer seemed to enjoy the pies, but the new assistant buyer that came with her hardly said or ate anything. I couldn't get a read on him."

"Or maybe you were reading too much into what he wasn't saying. It sounds like he was just the new guy tagging along. Stop worrying. You're just driving yourself crazy. Everybody loves your pies."

"I probably am making something out of nothing." And Philippa was right. Worrying didn't help. Rina went back to working on the order as she talked. "How are things going out there?"

"Busy. These days half the town is eating at the restaurant hoping to get a glimpse of the stars in the film. Too bad you couldn't stop by today. I saw your sexy stuntman at breakfast early this morning."

Rina added a case of spaghetti to the order. "He's not my sexy stuntman. Actually, I'll see him later. He's coming back by tonight to fix the sink in the ladies' room."

"He's what? No, reverse that. We'll get to why he's fixing the sink in a minute. Tell me about him coming back. When was he there the first time?"

Crap. That bit of info had just slipped out, but Philippa wasn't the type of friend to let it go. "Scott came in for dinner yesterday. The sink in the ladies' room sprang a huge leak while he was here, and he offered to fix it."

"And you said yes to a stranger. Wait, I guess he's not a stranger anymore. You're on a first-name basis now. So you said yes to *Scott* the sexy stuntman touching one of your precious sinks? Ooh, what's that all about?"

"Nothing." As Rina laughed, she glanced at the plastic bag on the dark gray padded chair across the desk with parts for the broken knob. "It's not a big deal. He feels guilty about smashing the pies and wants to make up for it by helping out. End of story. Time to change the subject."

"But…"

Another call buzzed in on Rina's phone. "I'd love to keep talking, but I gotta go. I'll call you later." Laughing, she ended the call with Philippa who was still objecting and answered the incoming one. "Hello."

"Hi, Rina. It's Linda from Gwen's Garden."

Rina immediately sat up straighter and dialed down from carefree to professional. "Hello, Linda. It's good to hear from you."

"Max and I really appreciate you setting up the tasting for us this morning. Your pies are amazing."

"Thank you." Rina fist pumped in her mind. "So what do you see as the next step?"

"Next steps. I'm glad you mentioned that."

Scott remained still as a makeup artist touched up the fake scar running from his right temple to his cheek. Coffee and a natural adrenaline rush had kept him going from the first scene of the day to what would now hopefully be his last—the stunt he and Kyle had rehearsed at the barn the day before when he'd run into Rina.

Instead of filming Nash's part in this scene separately from the stunts, the film's director, Holland Ainsley, had decided to shoot both at once. There definitely wouldn't be any interference this time. The area was completely blocked off from anyone except the cast and crew.

Outfitted similarly to him in a black cowboy hat, long dark duster coat, vest, pants and boots, Nash Moreland stood near the barn conferring with Kyle and Holland. At first glance, he and Nash looked alike—close in hair coloring, height and build, but unlike Nash, at age thirty-one Scott's face reflected a little more of life's experiences than the twenty-eight-year-old actor's.

As Holland led the conversation, she slid her mirrored aviators to the top of her hair that was gathered in an afro puff ponytail at the back of her head.

Dressed in a black vintage faded Metallica T-shirt, jeans and tan Lugz boots, she appeared casual, but the expression on her brown face reflected her intense focus on creating the best film possible.

The makeup artist finished and Scott adjusted the Stetson on his head. *Five more hours.* That's how long it was until he had to be at the cafe to help Rina. Maybe he'd make it there earlier. But that depended on Nash sticking to the script and not improvising or going off on another long tangent with Holland, exploring the motivation of the character he was playing—Montgomery, a futuristic gunslinger with telepathic abilities and superhuman strength.

Kyle waved Scott over to the group to join the conversation.

Holland looked to Nash. "We'll use a close-up of you standing on the beam." Her gaze moved to Scott. "But you'll do the swing-down."

Nash interjected, "I still think I should do the entire scene. It's not that complicated or dangerous."

Kyle shook his head. "Nope. Scott's already rehearsed it."

"It's just a swing-down," Nash insisted. "This whole scene is a piece of cake. I would have to do something really stupid or be clumsy as hell to get hurt."

Kyle's lips flattened and a tinge of red colored his face as he exchanged a "here we go again" look with Holland.

Scott briefly glanced down and stifled a chuckle.

Holland smiled at Nash. "We're going to let Kyle and Scott earn their money on this one. I really want you focused on capturing the mood of the scene after the swing-down happens." She turned to Scott. "After you land and roll, instead of drawing the pistol, I need you to take a knee and keep your head down." She looked back to Nash. "When you come back into the scene. You'll look up, engage the bad guys, and when you notice Bad Guy One getting away, you'll run to your horse."

Nash glanced between the front of the barn to a few yards away where a deep chestnut-colored horse stood with the trainer. "About halfway between the barn and the horse is when I should start to struggle because the evil-possessed sheriff is trying to hold me back with her power. The way I'm feeling this—my motivation is saving my family, but since I'm also still trying to conquer my own personal demons, that's the main reason I'm struggling to move forward. I'm vulnerable but I'm not willing to give up the fight."

Holland expertly navigated her back-and-forth with Nash, placating his need to find more meaning in the scene without taking up too much time. "I trust you," she added. "Follow your instincts."

Nash's expression grew more intense as he went off by himself to settle into character.

Meanwhile Scott rehearsed how Holland wanted him to roll into a crouched position on his knee, then climbed the metal scaffolding to the rafter.

Cameras and the operators behind them were positioned high and low in the barn to film multiple angles of the scene.

Once Kyle was satisfied that the cord was secure and the landing pads out in front of the barn were in place, "Quiet on the set," was called. Shortly after that Holland said, "Action!"

Scott leaped and grabbed the cord that was painted green. Special effects during the editing stage would change the color to a sparkling hue. As he swung through the air and out the barn, laser focus and muscle memory dictated his final moves. He landed, rolled and took a knee with his head down but slightly missed his mark.

Damn. Scott rose to his feet.

Holland sat behind the front camera. "That was good up until the end. Let's try that again."

Scott went back up the ladder. As he stood on the beam, he took a breath and blocked out all distractions. This time, when "action" was called and he went through the scene, he nailed the landing perfectly.

"Excellent." Holland nodded her approval.

Scott stepped out of camera range, watching as Nash took his place in front of the barn and mirrored the head-down crouched position.

The cameras started rolling and Nash slowly raised his head. In one quick movement, he stood, drew the prop six-shooter from the holster at his waist and fired. Small puffs of smoke rose from the gun as actors portraying the bad guys fired back.

Noticing the main bad guy getting away, Nash turned left and started running toward the horse. But instead of remaining still, as planned, the gelding started walking forward. Nash veered right to meet up with him, his legs and arms pumping at full speed…and tripped.

Chapter Eight

Rina searched through recipe websites on her computer. Fruit pies, chocolate pies, custard-based pies, but out of all of the recipes she'd searched through, nothing inspired her. Maybe because she couldn't stop her mind from wandering to Linda's call that afternoon about the tasting and the contract.

We have a few ideas we'd like to run by you…

As soon as she'd heard that line from Linda, she'd sensed something other than, "Congrats, I'm sending the documents right over" was coming, and she'd been right.

Max had felt her pies were too pedestrian for Gwen's Garden. He'd suggested the store have a separate line of pies, not the traditional fruit, nut or custard varieties served at the cafe, but flavors that were more unique. Linda still wanted to offer her the wholesaler's contract, but Rina would have to develop this new unique line that met their approval first. Another tasting for the new pies was scheduled in six weeks.

The clanging of dishes and pots as dinner service continued penetrated the closed door to the kitchen. Usually, she could tune out the noise, but tonight it fed the pain in Rina's temples that expanded and tightened like a band around her head.

Finding some pain reliever in her desk, she downed a pill with coffee. What about some sort of flavored cheesecake? But some people insisted it was a cake just because cake was in the name, and depending on the texture, others would insist it was a pie. Where would Max sit on the question? Just to be unique, he'd probably call it a tart.

An empty metal pot banged and rolled on the kitchen floor and as chatter from the staff grew louder, the pain in her temples grew worse.

She planted her hands on the desk and shoved up from the chair, ready to march into the kitchen and tell them to pipe down, but seconds before she did, Rina reined herself in. The dropped pot was an accident and not a reason for admonishment. A short temper was a sign she needed to leave. Rina turned off the computer, rolled back the desk chair and stood. She was going upstairs. After checking in with Ben about the status of the kitchen, she walked out to the dining area.

It was mostly full, but the staff wasn't slammed trying to keep up. In general, it wasn't bad for a Tuesday night.

She tracked down Darby restocking desserts in the showcase. "I'm going upstairs. You and Ben are in charge while I'm gone, and I'll also need you two to close up."

"Sure thing." Darby gave her a concerned look. "Everything okay?"

The burdens of the cafe didn't belong on the staff's shoulders. Rina conjured up a smile. "Yeah. Being her since six this morning has finally caught up with me. But if something comes up, I'm around."

"Alright, but we'll be fine. Oh, wait. What about the sink? Wasn't that guy coming back to fix it?"

The sink… She'd forgotten about that. Maybe Scott had, too. It was past eight thirty and he hadn't reached out to her. "Something must have come up and he couldn't make it. I'll call a plumber in the morning." So much for marking the sink from her to-do list.

Rina walked outside the front door of the cafe and breathed in the semicool air of a pleasant summer night.

Live music drifted from the wine bar farther down. Across the street, eight or nine high school kids were laughing and teasing each other in front of the ice cream parlor. A few doors down, a worker was setting up a new window display at the floral shop.

Instead of going upstairs, she turned to join the

few pedestrians strolling the sidewalks and ran into a human wall.

He grasped her arms and warmth along with a familiar spicy woodsy scent surrounded her. She looked up. "Scott. You came."

The boisterous teens from the ice cream parlor swarmed past.

She moved forward to get out of the way and her palm accidently landed on Scott's solid white fabric-covered chest.

He held her more securely. "Sorry I'm late. Something unexpected happened and I was held up. I would have called you, but things got hectic."

"It's okay. My day didn't go as planned either."

"What's going on?" He adjusted his stance.

His muscles shifting under Rina's palm woke her up to the fact that they were standing in the middle of the sidewalk, he was still holding her and she was touching him for no reason. Other than it felt comforting. With his size and solid strength, it was tempting to just stand there and lean into him.

Rina slipped back from his grasp and pushed out a breezy laugh. "I'm sure your day was a lot more interesting."

"Why would you think that?"

"Because working on a movie set seems like it would be much more exciting than events at the cafe."

He huffed a chuckle. "Some days more than others. Were you going someplace?"

"A short walk, but I have the parts for the sink. They're in my office."

"Do you mind if we don't go in yet?" He rolled his shoulders. "That walk actually sounds good. If you'd like some company."

His expression was easy to read. He needed some air just like she did. "Sure." She headed up the street away from the wine bar, walking toward the center of town.

As he matched his stride to hers, his movements were smooth and economical. Her jeans swished loudly as she walked while even with his heavy boots, he hardly made a sound.

In her mind's eye, she catalogued her face and the T-zone that was always an oil slick by the end of the day. And she'd forgotten to take off her apron. It was slightly rumpled and there was flour on her tennis shoes. Ugh! She looked terrible.

Her arm bumping his pulled her out of her thoughts. Or had he nudged her on purpose?

Scott smiled. "So tell me what happened?"

She waved him off. "Like I said, compared to your life, it's boring. Let's talk about your day instead."

They crossed the street to the bricked sidewalk surrounding the town square, a well-lit grassy area with a fountain in the center of it and park benches.

"How about a bet?" he asked. "You tell me about your day. I'll tell you about mine. Whoever's had the most intriguing day buys the ice cream."

"Sorry. I don't gamble."

"Not even for ice cream? Come on. Either way things shake out, it's a win."

The way he wiggled his eyebrows made Rina laugh. It was just a bet for ice cream not a wager on a race or a high-stakes poker game, and talking with him had already started to ease her headache. The possibility of complete relief from the pain loosed her words. "A few weeks ago, I was approached by a local natural foods store chain about providing pies for their stores."

"That's great. Congrats." He took a seat beside her on the park bench.

"Thank you." He'd been the first to congratulate her. Up until that moment, she hadn't really thought of just being approached by Gwen's Garden as an achievement. "But it's not as great as I thought it would be. I set up a tasting this morning. They like my pies but they want me to create a new dessert line for them."

"And the problem is?"

"The recipes for my pies have been in my family for decades." As she lifted her hands with a slight shrug, she searched for the words to explain. "They've been perfected over time. I just can't whip up a whole new line of different desserts in a few weeks."

"I don't know. To me, it sounds like *can't* isn't your problem. *Certainty* is."

"You lost me."

"Let me give you an example from my world."

He turned slightly toward her. "During my career, I've executed a thirty-foot-high jump from a stationary object several times. When I do it, I know exactly what I have to consider—height, speed, rate of impact. Those elements are a trusted part of the equation that will never change for me to make the perfect jump. In the same way, your family recipes have elements or ingredients combined in a certain way that you trust will make the perfect pie. Are you with me so far?"

"I guess. Truthfully, I'm still trying to imagine why anyone would willingly leap off a high stationary object."

His deep laugh was like a first sip of wine. Welcoming, relaxing and prompting her to sit back and enjoy the moment. "It's easy with the right safety equipment and precautions. But here's my point. If a director were to change the jump to forty or even fifty feet, the basic elements wouldn't change. Once the equipment and safety aspects are figured out, it comes down to me and how certain I am."

"And certainty comes with practice. And that's my problem with creating this new line. I don't have years, not even months to perfect things, just weeks."

"The first time I did a jump over thirty feet, I got one shot to get it right. And you know what?"

"You nailed it?" She couldn't stop a teasing smile as she tossed out what he'd said after nearly running her over in front of the barn,

"Good one." He chuckled. "But no. It wasn't perfect. It was ninety percent of what I wanted it to be but it was good enough for the director to keep in the film." Scott leaned in and interest along with an invisible tether wrapped round Rina and made her lean in, too. "Those pear bars you made yesterday, I'm guessing from your point of view, they're about ninety-five percent of what you'd like them to be."

"Try eighty."

"Personally, I thought they were on the money."

"Really?"

"Definitely." Scott looked into her eyes. "But I'm sure once you get them where you want them to be or create this new line, they'll be the right combination of sweetness and perfection."

"Thank you."

Perfection was the intensity in his gaze and the low-wattage version of his charming smile. It made her want to agree to anything he said just to keep looking at him and prolong the headiness and warmth expanding inside of her.

Yes, she understood what Scott was trying to tell her—that if she created the new line, what she deemed as almost good enough could actually be viewed as great in Max's and Linda's eyes. But why spend time creating desserts that they might not consider good enough? It wasn't like she needed the contract. No. Tomorrow, she was calling Linda and telling her she was taking a pass on creating the new line.

"Okay," Rina eased back a little. "I told you about

my day. Now it's your turn." As she sat back, Scott stretched his arm behind her.

"My day was great until this afternoon. Then it turned into chaos. Nash injured himself on set today. He tripped and ended up twisting his ankle and chipping a tooth."

"What? No way." She'd heard someone compare Nash to being a ten on the eye candy scale. It was hard to imagine him banged up, not that she'd really imagined him at all. "Is he going to be okay?"

"Probably. But the media and gossip from the set are his biggest worries now. Somebody tipped off the local paparazzi about what happened, and they showed up at the hospital. He and his publicist didn't feel comfortable with anyone seeing him injured so I got called in to act as a decoy. I pretended to be him coming out the front of the hospital so they could sneak him out the back."

"Did it work?"

"Yes. He's on his way to New York to see a specialist about his ankle and a cosmetic dentist to fix his tooth. I saw him at the hospital. He didn't look all that bad considering what happened, but his pride took a hit. He's embarrassed that he tripped running to get on a horse."

"Maybe it's a big deal for him because he's a celebrity, but everybody falls. My dad used to say falling was one of life's greatest lessons. I didn't see it then, but I do now. When you fall, you learn how to push past adversity and get up."

"That's exactly how I see it."

Great minds think alike. Rina stopped short of saying it aloud. The only reason she'd thought about it was because of the strong connection she felt with him. He probably didn't feel anything. She stood. "It's getting late. We should get back."

A look crossed his face as if he'd just remembered something. "Right, the sink." He rose to his feet. "The repair won't take long."

Feeling re-energized from her talk with Scott, she went back to her office instead of going to her apartment. While he worked, Rina began clearing files and recipe books from her desk. Linda had mentioned she was out of the office for the next few days. Sending a text declining the contract offer skirted the lines of unprofessional. She'd wait and give her a call on Monday.

Just as she tucked the last book on the shelf behind her desk, Scott rapped on the doorjamb. "I'm all done. Do you want to take a look?"

She followed him to the ladies' room and tried out the faucet. Water was flowing from where it should, and there were no leaks. And no reason for Scott to come back by.

Disappointment grew as Rina faced him. "Thank you for taking care of this, and thank you for listening to me earlier."

"No problem. And you won by the way. I owe you ice cream tomorrow."

"No. I owe *you* ice cream tomorrow. You having

to act as a decoy for Nash is a lot more intriguing than my situation."

He picked up the toolbox from the floor. "As a rule, I don't argue over ice cream so it's a date."

Giddy anticipation emerged, but Rina squashed it. They'd made a bet, she'd lost and was paying up in ice cream. That's all. It wasn't a date.

Chapter Nine

Philippa rapidly sliced a cucumber on a cutting board with a chef's knife. She paused a moment to look at Rina standing next to her at the silver prep table. "I hate to bust your bubble, but going out for ice cream—that's a date."

Between all of the happenings with the cafe and the situation with Gwen's Garden, of course, the topic Philippa was most interested in that morning was Scott. When Rina had mentioned she and Scott were going out for ice cream, Philippa had asked what she'd planned to wear and she'd said nothing special. After that, the date versus un-date debate kicked off.

In the midst of lunch service, cooks and kitchen helpers bustled around performing their tasks like clockwork in Pasture Lane Restaurant's red-tiled commercial kitchen.

Rina raised her voice over the cacophony, making sure Philippa heard her reply. "Scott and I made a bet, and I lost. Now I'm paying up in ice cream. That's not a date. It's a transaction."

"Let's see. A social engagement between two people, involving food, and the two people are attracted to each other." In one swift movement, Philippa gathered up the slices using the side of the knife and dropped them into a nearby bowl. "Definitely a date."

"Hold on. Who said Scott and I are attracted to each other?"

Philippa stared at her. "Do I really have to explain it to you? He made that bet, knowing either way he'd get to go out with you. A guy doesn't do that unless he's interested. I'll give him points for originality. But you get a side-eye for denying you didn't see it."

"But I didn't."

Philippa delivered the promised side-eye.

Rina stuck her hands in the front pocket of her purple apron stopping herself from throwing a cucumber at Philippa. "The point is, it's not a date because I don't consider it to be one."

"There are people in town who would be thrilled to be in your so-called un-date situation. Honestly, I don't understand why it's such a problem for you to go out with him."

"I didn't say it was a problem just a bad idea."

"Why?"

Last night on the park bench with Scott, the way they'd gotten along so easily and how she'd confided in him so quickly—she'd experienced that only one other time. Falling hard and fast for Xavier had been her first mistake, and she wouldn't repeat it with Scott. But if she admitted that, Philippa would want to dive deeper into it. Something she didn't want to do in public and didn't have time for since she was meeting Zurie soon.

Rina checked the time on her phone. "Dating requires energy and commitment, and I'm a hundred percent committed to Brewed Haven."

"One date isn't a long-term commitment. Unless it's so good and you decide to indulge. Then it might be longer."

Rina could feel the glances from some of the staff, now curious about her and Philippa's discussion while others were seemingly engrossed in finding pots or utensils on a nearby rack. "Again, it's not a date, and can we not talk about *indulging* right now in front of everyone?"

"Yes, but it shouldn't matter what we're talking about," Philippa spoke louder. "Because instead of ear-hustling our conversation, my capable staff should be busy making sure we have enough baked potatoes prepped for dinner so we don't run out of them like we did last night."

Someone standing near the rack dropped a metal pan and like a horn at a starting line, everyone around them reanimated, fully interested in their work.

Philippa went back to her cucumbers. "Would it be so hard not to overcomplicate the situation and just go out with him?"

"I'm not overcomplicating the situation. There are plenty of good reasons why I shouldn't." Her phoned buzzed in with a text. "It's Zurie. She wants to meet earlier. I have to go."

"See you later. And for the record, when it comes to the whole dating thing, I'm a hundred percent team Scott."

"Gee, bestie, thanks for the support."

Philippa shrugged off the sarcasm. "You're welcome."

As Rina headed for the double doors leading to the dining room of Pasture Lane, she put the date versus un-date debate to rest. Aside from the issue of Scott being a little too easy to like, dating, having a good time, indulging, whatever Philippa wanted to call it, all took effort. If she was going to put effort into anything, her choice was Brewed Haven. After five years in business, she was finally reaping some rewards for her hard work. This was the time to keep building, not to get sidetracked by distractions. *Listen to me, sounding like a seasoned boss.* Rina laughed silently.

Her first year in business, she'd practically worn herself out trying to get the cafe off the ground. She'd also learned what it took to be a business owner. Year two, she'd had a couple of bad breaks and struggled financially but she'd made it through. Years three and four, she'd kept building Brewed Haven to where it was now—a thriving business with a strong foothold in the community.

Rina stepped into the half-full dining area.

Guests and local customers sat at wood tables with green padded chairs enjoying a leisurely breakfast. Zurie walked in on the other side of the room near the hostess station, and her presence drew several people's attention away from the lush green scenery outside the wall of glass.

Compared to Rina's casual attire of a Brewed Haven T-shirt, apron and jeans, Zurie looked the part of an efficient office executive in a white blouse, navy skirt and matching pumps. Her dark hair was loose around her shoulders.

Rina met her in the center of the restaurant. Despite their almost nine year age difference, Zurie looked younger. Years ago, when they were both in their twenties, more than a few people had assumed Zurie was her more serious fraternal twin. Many people had also viewed Zurie as the more responsible one back then. Sometimes it felt like Zurie still did.

"Good, you're here." Zurie glanced down and tapped into her phone. "Let's talk in my office."

Rina opened her mouth to ask if she could grab a coffee first, but Zurie was already halfway to the entrance. She followed her out.

In the corridor behind the lobby of the guesthouse,

staff in blue uniform coveralls cleaned the restrooms and straightened the gold-tiered literature stand filled with tourist brochures.

A little farther down, a shorter hallway to the right led to the business center, a meeting space and the fitness room.

Just as they walked past the hallway, someone called out, "Rina!"

She stepped back to see who it was.

Halfway down, Scott looked in her direction, smiling as he filled a gray bottle at the water fountain. "Wait up." He screwed the top on the bottle.

As Scott jogged toward her, a blond woman heading into the business center paused to take in the view.

In a black tank top, his chest and shoulders seemed wider and his arms more defined. Loose gray shorts revealed his muscular legs.

Noticing the woman's mouth remained opened as she stared, Rina shut hers.

Scott stopped in front of her. Wisps of damp hair stuck to his forehead. "Hey. How are you?"

Up close, the view was even more impressive. "Hi. Were you in the gym? Of course you were." Did she just do the answering her own questions thing? But she'd outgrown that nervous habit years ago.

"Yeah, had to get in a workout." He moved closer and the clean scent of soap and the faint hint of sweat, the good kind, wafted in her direction. "Are we still on for tonight?"

Rina automatically moved closer to him. *Attraction.* Philippa proclaiming that as part of the date scenario pinged loudly in her mind, and Rina took a step back. "Yes. Our appointment is still on." Since it wasn't a date, that was the perfect word to call it.

His eyes narrowed a bit with a quizzical look and then his gaze shifted past her shoulder. He smiled politely at Zurie then looked back at Rina. "Right, so about our appointment, I can actually come by earlier or we can meet after Brewed Haven closes. There's been some changes on set. My schedule has freed up."

Zurie's heels tapped on the tiles as she shifted her stance reminding Rina she was still waiting… and listening. "No. Eight is great. Thanks. I'll see you then."

She turned and joined Zurie. At eight thirty she would use the excuse of needing to get back to the cafe for closing to bring their "appointment" to an end. A clearly defined time frame that was less than an hour—she was adding that one to the rules about what *wasn't* a date.

As they walked briskly down the corridor, Zurie looked at her phone. "Now we're back down to a fifteen-minute meeting, maybe I can squeeze in twenty. That guy, he's part of the film crew, isn't he? What type of appointment do you have with him?"

"We're discussing some minor repair stuff at the cafe." That wasn't a lie. Just a vague explanation that shouldn't open the topic up to more scrutiny.

"Isn't Dennis handling repairs?"

The door to potential criticism widened. An object high in the left corner, and the perfect deflection, caught Rina's attention. She smiled. "When did you install a new security camera?"

Zurie glanced up at it as she slid a card into the reader above the door handle. "A few weeks ago." The locking mechanism disengaged and she opened the door. "I don't know if anyone told you, but we had a scare awhile back when a little boy ran off from his father. Afterward, we decided the security here and at the stable needed an upgrade."

Rina followed her into the office. Relieved the topic had moved from more questions about her appointment with Scott, she settled in one of the blue chairs in front of the oak desk. "Philippa mentioned that happened. Didn't Tristan and Chloe find him?"

"Yes, they did. We were lucky the boy's disappearance didn't escalate to an even more serious issue."

Zurie put her phone down as she sat behind the desk in a large brown leather chair that had belonged to their father. The top of her workspace was uncluttered and neat with just a wide-screen computer, a cube of tissues and a filled outbox on one top corner and a less full inbox on the other. The only other furniture was a round meeting table with black padded chairs at the other end of the room, and also a new addition since Rina had been in the office several weeks ago—a navy couch along the far wall.

With the tinted window behind her providing a view of one of the pastures, Zurie completely lived up to the image of being in charge. Their father had seemed larger than life too when he'd sat in that chair.

A vision of him at his desk in his office that had been in their family home came into Rina's mind. As a little girl, she used to stop in and bug him at least once a day and he'd never gotten angry with her.

Hey, Sweet Pea...

That's what he'd say when he spotted her in the doorway. His huge laugh had always filled the room and she'd loved hearing it. As she poked around his desk playing with his pens and pencils, he'd pretend that he didn't realize her main objective was candy. Then he'd distract her, and suddenly his Jolly Rancher stash would appear on his desk. She loved the apple-flavored ones, and he always seemed to have more of those than any of the others.

"Did you hear what I said?" Zurie stared at her.

Rina reluctantly let go of the memory of their father and focused on the conversation. "Sorry. Can you repeat it?"

"Let me guess. You weren't listening because you were daydreaming about your *appointment*?"

From the lack of amusement in Zurie's expression, she wouldn't believe that she was actually thinking about their father so what was the point of saying it. "I'm listening now."

"I got a call from the production company last

night and a follow-up email this morning. Nash Moreland injured himself yesterday. Everything is on hold until they sort out when he's coming back."

"Oh?" The production shutting down for a while, was that why Scott's time had freed up? "So will the cast and crew still be around?"

"That's undecided." Zurie sank back in the chair. "If the set is shut down longer than a week, they'll send everyone home. But every day they're not filming is costing them money and us, too. All catering for the cast and crew has been suspended until further notice. And when they do go back into full production, catering may be stripped down to the essentials. Your pies are considered a luxury." A brief flash of empathy shown in Zurie's eyes. "There's a strong chance your month-to-month contract may not be renewed."

Disappointment dropped inside of Rina and she sank back in her seat. She'd been counting on that contract to buy some new equipment. Strange. Zurie had said they sent out a message. She hadn't seen it. "I must have skipped over the email that went out. I'll look for it."

"They didn't send it to you. I told them they didn't need to because I'd keep you informed about what's happening."

But her contract was with the company not Zurie. She should have been cc'd on the correspondence. Why had Zurie butted in? Irritation started to rise inside of Rina. But knowing Zurie, offering to tell her about the situation was problem solving not a slight. Complaining about it would make her sound petty instead of professional. "Thanks for telling me about the changes. Can you send me a copy of the email, please?"

"Sure." Zurie picked up her phone from the desk.

A chime rang on Rina's phone. She'd reach out to the contact person and ask them to add her to the email chain. "Thanks for keeping me in the loop. I should head back to work."

"Wait." Zurie stalled her from getting up with a raised hand. "The contract isn't all I wanted to talk to you about."

Chapter Ten

Scott walked into Brewed Haven, and from the looks of things, it was fairly busy. Good food, great desserts and coffee—he could understand why it would be a popular spot on a Wednesday night.

Darby came out of the archway next to the counter carrying a tray of sodas. He waited until she dropped them off to customers, then approached her.

Recognizing him, Darby smiled. "Hi, Scott." Her gaze moved down and up over his black button-down, dark jeans and black Timberlands. "Are you here for dinner?"

"Actually, I'm looking for Rina."

"She's in her office." Darby led the way to the corridor. A crash of plates in the dining area made her grimace. "You know the way." She pointed left as she started across the dining room. "First door on the right. Just knock before you go in."

As he entered the corridor, servers rushed by him to pick up food from the service window farther up on the right and to dispense sodas from the beverage machine across from it.

Scott rapped on the office door a couple of times then slowly cracked it open. "Rina, it's Scott." He peeked in.

She wasn't there. A large stack of books and a file folder indicated she'd been working there at some point.

Glancing out the large window looking out on the kitchen, he saw Rina with a bright yellow hairnet covering her braids. She and a young woman peered into a stock pot on the stove. Using a plastic spoon, Rina sampled the contents of the pot then spoke to the woman who nodded agreeably at whatever she was saying.

As Rina tossed the spoon into a nearby trash can, she spotted him through the window and gestured for him to wait one minute.

Scott nodded. He glanced at her full desk. Hopefully she wasn't too busy to get away.

A few moments later, she came into the office through the kitchen door. "Sorry for making you wait. We ran out of chicken soup and had to make another batch." She glanced at him on the way behind her desk. "You look nice."

"Thanks."

Honestly, he'd made an effort. When he'd talked to her in the hallway that morning, he'd just completed a light twenty-minute warm-up sprint on the elliptical. The way she'd backed away and abruptly ended their conversation had made him wonder if he'd offended her by being too sweaty. Impressing her was important. Although going for ice cream was part of a bet, technically, it was their first time going out together. And if he had any say in the matter, it wouldn't be their last.

Rina took off the hairnet and apron, laid both on her desk, then snagged her phone from the top drawer. She seemed preoccupied. "I'm ready."

As he followed her out, she slipped her hand into her back pocket and pulled out some folded money. He was going to tell her she didn't need it, but he couldn't tear his attention from the way her jeans clung to her curves.

Outside, she picked up the pace to the opposite sidewalk.

With his longer legs, he easily strode beside her. "So how's your day been?"

Rina smiled up at him. "Is that question part of another bet?"

"No, because I'd lose. Your life is lot more fascinating than mine."

She laughed ruefully. "Today, I'd settle for boring."

Before he could ask why, they arrived at their destination and went inside. She ordered a small cup of chocolate cookie dough ice cream. He got a mint chocolate chip cone.

Rina handed the cashier her money before he could get his wallet out.

That's okay, he'd pay the next time.

The well-lit space wasn't full, but people were spread throughout the small seating area. One group in the middle were laughing and talking loudly.

"Can w—" Scott and Rina both spoke at the same time.

"You first," he said.

"Can we walk instead of staying in here?"

That's almost exactly what he'd planned to ask. "Great minds think alike."

As she grabbed a few napkins from a dispenser on the counter, she gave him a quizzical look. "I guess they do."

Outside, on the sidewalk, they weren't practically running a marathon like they were on the way to the ice cream place, but she wasn't talking or eating.

He licked his cone. "Is your ice cream okay?"

"It's fine."

"Busy day?"

"The usual. What about you? What are you doing now that filming is on hold?"

She was really good at changing the subject away from herself. He'd let her get away with it for now, but he really didn't want to spend the entire time talking about himself. He wanted to know more about her. "A lot of sitting and waiting, at least for the rest of this week."

"If it turns out to be longer, will you go home?"

He walked with her across the street to the town square. "That depends on how long. Right now, the director and the main production crew are determining if they can shoot around Nash until he gets back."

"But you're his stunt double. How would that work for you if he's not around?"

"Even during a regular production schedule, Nash and I aren't always working together. There's a first unit or filming team that works with the main actors. The second unit films stunts and other scenes not involving them. When I'm not filming, I help Kyle and the other stunt performers with setups and rehearsals. Or if background extras are needed, sometimes I fill in there, too."

They dropped down on the same bench they'd sat on the day before, facing the fountain.

She went quiet again.

At Tillbridge, she'd called going out for ice cream with him an appointment. Appointments often involved things people felt they *had* to do, not wanted to do. Did Rina feel obligated to go out with him because of their friendly bet or because he'd put her on the spot in the hallway by asking about it? Maybe she wasn't eating her ice cream because she didn't want to be there with him.

Just as he was about to ask Rina if she wanted

to go back to the cafe, she asked, "How did you become a stuntman?"

He'd answered that question in polite conversations more times than he could count, but the sincere expression on her face prompted him to settle back on the bench. "A guy I was serving with in the navy thought he was the next Brad Pitt. When we were both honorably discharged in San Diego, he talked me into going with him to LA. Shortly after we got there, he won a part in a commercial, and I went with him to the filming. The acting part of things didn't interest me, but what the stuntman was doing caught my attention so I talked to him, and he turned me on to a place offering stunt training. After that, it took some time to establish myself, but I did, and I haven't stopped working since."

"Is your friend still acting?"

"No. He eventually focused on his personal training business and invested in a gym with his brother."

"So after the navy, you had no interest at all in joining your family's business?"

"Not really." He licked melting ice cream from the side of the cone. "I'd been gone for four years. My sister, Wendy, had been working her tail off helping my father build the company. She's also highly organized and tenacious, and she loves corporate structure. I don't." He shrugged not knowing quite how to explain something that had felt like such a natural decision to him. "Even though I wasn't sure what I wanted to do after the navy, I knew working for my father wasn't the right thing for me. But as his son, the expectation was that I would. My showing up would have just gotten in the way of Wendy establishing herself as the boss. I didn't want that for her."

Once again, she looked at him as if she was almost troubled by what he'd said. He couldn't get a read on her. What was she thinking?

He turned partially and faced her. "Okay, that's the second time you've done that. What's up?"

She raised her brows at him. "Done what?"

"Given me a strange look. You've also been really quiet. Either I've got ice cream on my face or something is on your mind."

Chapter Eleven

Rina stared back at him. Amusement but also a tiny bit of exasperation shown on his face. From his point of view, she couldn't blame him. If he'd been giving her strange looks and not saying much, she'd wonder what was wrong, too.

"I'm sorry. I didn't mean to act weird." Rina stuffed her napkins into her ice cream and set the cup between them on the bench. "It's just that when we were in the ice cream shop, you said great minds think alike and that was the same thing I thought the other day when you'd said something. And just now, when you mentioned not wanting to ruin things for your sister at your father's company, it reminded me of something Tristan did for my sister Zurie."

"So our similarities on a few things bothers you?"

"No. I just haven't had a conversation with someone where there so many coincidences. Even the organized and tenacious part you mentioned about your sister, fits my sister, too."

"Does she also like to butt in, take control and give opinions about your life?"

"Exactly."

He chuckled wryly and stuck the remainder of his cone in her cup. "Our sisters sound like long lost twins."

"You're right. They do." Two people like Zurie in the world? That was a bit much. She loved Zurie, but...

Scott leaned toward her. "That part about our sisters being twins was supposed to make you laugh. Since you're not, I'm guessing something happened between you and her today."

Comparing experiences with their sisters was one thing, but telling him, a guy she barely knew, about the details of her meeting with Zurie? She couldn't. She shouldn't. But she couldn't talk to Tristan. Something his father had done was part of the situation, and Tristan might feel he needed to get involved. Talking to Philippa about what she and Zurie had discussed was probably more appropriate. Actually, it hadn't been a discussion. Zurie had dictated the solution and expected her to agree to it.

Rina released a long breath filled with frustration. But she really needed to talk right then and Scott was there. Maybe it would be easier to share what was going on with someone who didn't know all of the details about her past mistakes. "Brewed Haven was my first big venture, and I was determined to make it the place of my dreams."

He turned, angling his body more toward her. "There's nothing wrong with that. A lot of people feel that way about their first business."

"Well, my dreams weren't inexpensive. When I had to make a choice between leasing one of the new spaces next to the flower shop or buying the building where a bakery used to be, I bought the building. Maybe I should have torn it down and started from scratch, but to me fixing up the place was like a phoenix rising from the ashes." Kind of how she envisioned herself after the accident. Rina caught herself rubbing over her right knee.

Scott noticed, too. From his expression, he'd made the connection between what she was and wasn't telling him. "You've done a great job rebuilding things."

"Thank you. But there were consequences to spending so much up front. I didn't have enough cash in reserve. Two years in, a storm came through, and there was a lot of damage. Insurance covered a good part of it, but I didn't have the resources to rebuild plus run the cafe." A shadow of feeling like a failure that she'd felt then fell over her now. "I missed a few loan payments, and I was too embarrassed to tell anyone about it."

"But you worked it out." He pointed to the cafe behind them. "Brewed Haven is still standing."

"Only because I had help. One of the loan officers at the bank was good friends with my uncle, Jacob. He told my uncle I was in trouble. I should have been upset that the loan officer shared the information, but honestly, I was relieved…and scared. I'd put everything into Brewed Haven and didn't want to lose it. Uncle Jacob gave me the money to rebuild and catch up. He'd said it was a gift and to keep it between us. But yesterday, Zurie told me he hadn't used his personal money. He'd borrowed it from the family corporation that Tillbridge falls under. All this time, it was misclassified on the balance sheets by our old accountant. Zurie recently switched firms, and they found it during their audit. So instead of being caught up, I'm in debt to Tillbridge."

"Wait." He leaned in. "Your sister isn't expecting you to repay the money, is she?"

The judgment on Zurie's face had conveyed her thoughts so clearly, it had been as if Rina could read her mind— *This wouldn't have happened if you'd made better choices and not bought that building.*

"No, but I'm the reason the loan exists. It should be my responsibility. I refuse to be treated like a charity case."

"Can you handle paying the loan without jeopardizing the business?"

"Yes. At least I can once I win the Gwen's Garden contract."

"You didn't seem too enthused about doing it the last time we talked."

"Enthusiasm isn't going to pay off my loan. Like you said, I just have to get used to creating something that's different from my usual." And all that required was her getting over feeling like she was jumping into the deepest part of a lake.

Scott blew out a breath. "I know doing what you have to do isn't always easy. I wish I could help."

Actually Scott already had. He hadn't offered an unwanted opinion, and he'd allowed her to express exactly how she felt about the situation—frustrated and sad.

She glanced at their melted ice creams. "Sorry for ruining going out tonight."

"You didn't. I asked what was wrong and you needed to talk. But if you feel that strongly about it, we'll just make another appointment and do this again."

His small teasing smile prompted a laugh out of her. "I'd like that." It was only fair since she'd spent their time together talking about another not-so-happy moment in her life.

In silent agreement they stood, and she waited for him as he threw the ice cream cup away.

As she started to cross the street, he lightly grasped her arm, stalling her. "I understand how curveballs can really throw things off when you're running a business. I watched my father deal with more than a few. If you need to talk again, I'm here to listen, ice cream appointment or not."

"Thank you." The empathy in his gaze prompted

her to kiss his cheek. The smoothness of his skin and the wonderful smell of his cologne caused her to linger. Scott turned to look at her, and what she saw in his eyes suspended her even longer.

As their lips hovered a hairsbreadth apart, anticipation flowed through the current that hummed between them in that tiny space, overpowering reason and hesitation. She pressed her lips to his. The contact awakened something that took notice and grabbed hold of her. Rina opened to him and the flavors of chocolate, mint, and the slow drift and glide as they deepened the kiss grew addictive. The need to get closer bloomed inside of her, and she slid her hands up and around his neck. As he grasped her waist and brought her against him, she welcomed the contact with a sigh. *Yes.* Lost in what she couldn't define, Rina knew she just wanted more.

A car horn blared. Tires squealed. The sounds scratched the surface of a recollection and yanked her back to reality.

Scott's arms went around her as they both looked up the street.

Two cars crossing into the intersection at the same time had narrowly avoided a collision, but the image in front of Rina was cluttered by her own elusive memories jumbled with a mix of terrible emotions.

She sucked in a breath filled with Scott's scent. Without realizing it, she'd closed her eyes and burrowed her face into his chest.

"Are you okay? You're shaking." Scott, his arms now completely wrapped around her, tightened his hold.

Stay. Soak up his warmth and his strength. That's what every part of her screamed out. But something about helplessness sucking her down and leaning on someone for comfort was all too familiar. Years ago, vulnerability had gotten the best of her, and needing an escape from reality, she'd found it in Xavier's arms.

Feeling almost as if she was in the repeat of a dream she had to wake up from but wished she didn't, Rina looked up at him. "I think that was my signal to go back to work."

"The kiss or the near wreck?"

"Both." She moved back. "The cafe is my priority." Testing uncharted waters, she ventured out. "So can we leave that kiss as just a kiss?"

He studied her a moment. "If that's what you want. Just so you know, I'm not following you. I have ice cream on my hands. I need to wash it off."

"Of course."

Inside the cafe, as Rina headed to her office, she struggled not to look back at him. No matter how much she liked kissing him, viewing that moment as "just a kiss" was the smartest thing to do.

Sitting at her desk, she pulled up his number on her phone. She didn't need it anymore. Her finger hovered over the delete icon.

A knock sounded at the corridor-side door.

"Come in."

Scott walked inside. "Got a minute? There's an issue with the men's room."

The troubled look on his face almost made Rina want to crawl under her desk. "What type of issue?"

"It's probably best for you to see it yourself."

She followed him. *Please, not another broken sink.*

After a quick peek to make sure the bathroom wasn't occupied, he beckoned her inside and pointed to a water stain on the ceiling above the sinks that hadn't been there a couple of days ago. "What's up there?"

Rina visualized the floor plan of her apartment. Her heart sank.

Chapter Twelve

As she stood in front of the bathroom mirror in her apartment, Rina gathered her braids into a ponytail. The soothing scents of clary sage, lavender and sweet almond moisturizer calmed her. But as her gaze drifted to the claw-foot tub with silver feet on the other side of the room, peace evaporated.

The second contractor she'd hired a little over five years ago to help with the apartment remodel had understood her vision of not wanting a traditional shower and tub area. He'd put a sloping drain in the beige tile floor near the claw-foot tub, tiled the walls partway surrounding it and installed a showerhead, and she'd painted the space a soothing blue. When her bathroom sanctuary was completed, her heart had leaped high on the excitement meter. But now, relaxing herbal-infused soaks or long hot showers in her favorite spot were on hold. Scott believed a faulty pipe, somewhere behind the showerhead wall, was causing a leak in the men's bathroom downstairs.

The ringtone she'd assigned to Philippa, "Lean On" by Major Lazer and DJ Snake, blasted from her phone. After wiping her hands on a coral hand towel, she hurried out of the corner bathroom, snagged the phone from the polished wood dresser and answered it. "Hey."

"Good morning," Philippa sang out. "I have a whole ten minutes before I have to leave my office and go to the kitchen. Tell me about your date."

"You may have time but I still have to get ready for work." She still needed to get dressed.

"You can't leave me in suspense all day. Just give me the highlights."

I kissed him. But trying to explain to Philippa that it was just a kiss and didn't validate her date theory would take more than ten minutes.

Rina flopped back on the queen-sized sleigh bed. With the low light peeking through the blinds over the wide side window, it would be so easy to snuggle back under the tousled cream sheets and forget she had a cafe to run. "Let's see. The highlights. It wasn't a date. We had ice cream, and when we came back to the cafe, he noticed a leak in the men's room ceiling. My shower is causing it."

"What is up with the two of you and water?"

"There's nothing up with the two of us. It's an old building."

"But you didn't have these problems until he showed up."

"Are you saying he's cursed?" Maybe he was. When they kissed an accident *did* almost happen.

"No, he's too cute to be cursed. Maybe it's ghosts in the plumbing."

As Rina got up, she switched to speaker mode. "Seriously? After everything I just told you, haunted water pipes is what you come up with?"

"It's more interesting than old leaky pipes. You know, I read a romance novel about a haunted mansion once…"

Philippa went on to describe the entire plot about ghosts who were lovers when they'd been alive but had ended up trapped by a curse keeping them from being together in the afterlife.

Rina found a pair of jeans in the closet and put them on. As she walked into the living room, natural light from the large tinted windows on the side wall bathed the dark-wood furniture, cream couch with turquoise pillows, and matching side chairs in a soft glow.

A stop in the laundry room in the side hallway netted her clean socks. Farther up, as she passed the kitchen, she snagged her keys off the white marble counter.

In the entryway, as she slipped on her tennis shoes, Philippa finally took a breath allowing Rina to comment. "I still don't understand what that story has to do with me. I own a cafe with glitchy plumbing not a mansion."

"But you do have a hot handyman. And just like in the book, you two could fall in love and the ghosts who are messing with your plumbing could live happily-ever-after."

A laugh slipped out of Rina as she disengaged the alarm on the wall panel. Only Philippa would try to connect that story to her life. "Ghosts are not haunting my plumbing, and I'm not going to fall in love with my hot handyman. Drool over him, definitely, but..." Rina opened the front door and smacked into said handyman's gaze. "Scott."

"But Scott, what? Let me guess. Doing anything with him is a bad idea? Girl, you need to let that go and do exactly what I told you to do. Indulge. If you need convincing, just imagine him with his shirt off."

Scott's brows rose.

Rina hung up on Philippa.

Scott grinned as he set the toolbox on the cream counter in Rina's bathroom. A moment ago, after pointing him in the right direction, she'd rushed out the door.

Of course he'd wanted to know more about what he'd overheard before and after she'd opened the door, but from the cute look of embarrassment on her face, he wasn't getting that answer.

Last night, after Rina had insisted they view their

kiss as "just a kiss," he'd wondered if they would ever spend time together again. He'd also been concerned about misreading her. She'd kissed him, but she'd also been a little vulnerable over finding out about the loan from her sister. Instead of going all in on the kiss should he have been the one to ease up?

Bottom line, Rina had made her position clear. She didn't want to take things further. He'd planned to clear the air about it this morning, and let her know he was good just helping out as the repairman. But if she asked him, he'd gladly take his shirt off for her. She'd said he was hot. Scott couldn't stop a widening grin. But she might feel differently if he didn't get this repair right.

He hadn't done a job like this in a while, but he could get it done. Still, it would be great to run through the steps with someone who did this type of work more often than he did. Scott pulled up the familiar number but instead of voice he chose video.

After a couple of rings, a close-up image of Wendy's face appeared on the screen. Her dark blond waves flowed back from her slim face. The freckles across her nose indicated she'd recently been out in the Florida sun. "Hey, you."

"Got a minute?"

"Sure, as long as I can sit and drink coffee while we talk." She dropped down on what appeared to be a step on a wooden staircase.

"Where are you?"

"Visiting one of our project sites. It's a house

that's being renovated. It's a beauty. I'm meeting the owner to go over a few designs, but he's running late. What do you need?"

"Advice. I think a friend has a leak in their bathroom wall. I wanted you to take a look and walk through the repair with me before I did anything."

"Sure." She slipped a pair of glasses down from the top of her head and positioned them over her light hazel-brown eyes. "Show me."

He switched the camera view from him to the tub area.

"That's a smart design for a claw-foot tub. But if I would have done it, I would have brought the tile walls farther up. What makes you think there's a leak in the wall?"

Scott explained about the cafe and what he'd noticed in the men's room.

Wendy nodded. "That sounds reasonable, but I'd still use a moisture finder to make sure the numbers line up with the leak coming from the shower and not some other random place. If it's an older building, there could be some weird pipe configurations."

"Good to know."

"Then I'd..." She looked up from the phone. "I think the owner is driving up."

"Can we talk after your meeting?"

"Dad." She called out behind her up the stairs. "Scott has a question about a shower repair. I have to meet with our client. Can you talk to him?"

"Wendy, no, I can call you back."

The camera view had already changed to her climbing the stairs.

Was she really trying to help him out or was she setting up another chance for his father to ask him to come to his wedding?

Patrick Halsey's face appeared on the screen. Scott had his father's eyes and at one time he'd had his perfectly straight nose, but a wild punch thrown during a fight scene brawl had left his with a small bump. His father grinned, happy to see him. "Hi. Wendy said you have a question about something?"

His father was even more knowledgeable than Wendy. Talking to him would only be a benefit. He told his father the same thing he'd outlined for Wendy and what she'd mentioned so far. "Yes, she's definitely right about the pipe configurations in the wall." Like Wendy, he slid his glasses from the top of his head to his nose. "Can you give me a closer look at the wall where the showerhead is and then the faucet assembly?"

He showed his father what he'd asked, and they talked through the repair and what to look out for. It was like old times when he'd used to work for him. Before Scott realized it, they'd been on the phone for almost thirty minutes talking about the repair and issues his father had encountered working on similar jobs. "Thanks, Dad. I appreciate the assist."

"Wish I was there to help. Like I said, my money is on a broken backflow valve. Older buildings can be a headache but also a nice challenge. Where did you say this place was?"

Scott hesitated.

Wendy's smiling face suddenly appeared next to his father's. "So did you two figure it out?"

"I think we did," his father replied. "I better get going. I'm supposed to meet Theresa at the florist. Good luck. Let me know what you find."

"I will. Thanks, Dad."

His father left the screen and only Wendy remained. "So things must be slow on set with the movie since you have time for side gigs."

"Today, yes. Tomorrow…"

"Let me guess. You'll be busy?" She glanced over her shoulder then back at the screen. "Liar-liar-pants-on-fire. I saw the story online about Nash. He broke his nose and his leg. Filming's going to be shut down for weeks, maybe months, giving you plenty of time to repair that shower and make it to Dad's wedding."

"You must have gotten that from one of those tabloid sites. Nash chipped a tooth and he sprained his ankle. Most likely, the director is going to film around him until he's able to come back in a few weeks."

"Whatever's happening, it sounds like you have the time to come to the ceremony. Dad won't say it, but I know he's really disappointed that you won't be here."

Guilt started to rise, but his reasoning about not wanting to go through another one of his father's weddings overrode it. "I don't have a say in the filming schedule. I have to be available when they need me."

As Wendy stared at him she released a breath. "Can't you at least try to work something out…for his sake?"

Chapter Thirteen

Rina stood outside the door of her apartment holding a large foil-covered plate and saucer. She'd been out there for at least a good two minutes debating whether or not to go inside and face Scott. But after he'd heard her and Philippa talking about him earlier that morning, how could she?

He'd sent a text a couple of hours ago, wanting to talk to her about what he planned to do in her bathroom. She'd texted back that she was busy, and that he should go ahead with the repair and bill her for his time and the supplies. To make sure she didn't have to see him, she'd even sent Darby to give him the spare key so he could get in and out of the apartment without her.

Once again, the moment from that morning of

opening the door and Philippa telling her to imagine him with his shirt off played in her mind. Rina groaned and started descending the steps with the metal grill–style railing on the side of the building. But halfway down she went back up. She had to go inside some time, not only because she lived there, but to check on what he was doing. Her entire apartment could be a construction zone by now, and she'd sanctioned it with her texts.

Leaning against the wall in the entryway, she toed off her tennis shoes near the door.

A Maroon 5 song blared from the back hall.

After leaving the plate and saucer in the kitchen, she followed the music to her bathroom. Bracing herself for maximum damage, she peeked inside.

Plastic draping lay on the floor around the tub and a thick blanket-like drape covered it.

Scott stood in the tub singing and humming to the song as he used a small saw-like tool to cut through the drywall below the showerhead.

He paused to wipe his brow with the hem of his blue shirt, and Rina's imagination went rogue.

Endless abs. That's what was probably under his shirt.

He went back to work.

Rina erased the vision. "Hey, can we talk?"

Scott jerked his hand away from the wall and cursed.

Crap! She hurried to him. "How bad is it?"

"I'll live." Scott set the tool down near his feet

and snatched up a worn faded green rag from the side of the tub.

She grabbed his arm before he pressed it to his wound. "Don't use that. It's not clean. Hold on." Rina lifted his hand above his head. "Keep it there."

As he followed her instructions, he leaned down to his phone lying in the bottom of the tub and turned off the music. "It's not that big of a deal."

"Anytime there's blood, it's a big deal. Broken skin can get infected." She found the first aid kit in the cabinet below the sink and set it on the counter. After digging out packets of alcohol wipes, she turned to him. "Let me see."

He lowered his arm and she took his hand. A series of small cuts ran along the knuckles of his thumb and index finger.

She removed the dampened gauze from the packet and dabbed it over his wounds.

He flinched. "That hurts."

"I thought this wasn't a big deal." She blew softly over his hand and kept cleaning the cuts.

"It wasn't until you touched it."

The husky tone in Scott's voice made her look up. Her heart tripped. Resisting falling into his lazy smile, she went back to the first aid kit and returned with two large Band-Aids. "Just make sure you play nice with sharp objects from now on."

"Give me a break. You snuck up on me."

"I'm sorry." She opened one of the adhesive

bandages and wound it around his index finger. "I shouldn't have walked up on you like that."

"I'll accept your apology on one condition." He caught her hand making her pause in wrapping his thumb. "Stop avoiding me. I'm starting to feel like I'm invading your space instead of helping you out."

The earnestness in his eyes raised remorse. "Actually that's why I came up here. I brought you breakfast. I thought we could talk."

"About you wanting to take my clothes off?"

"I don't."

"That's not what I heard." A teasing smile played over his kissable mouth.

She bobbled the bandage and momentarily stuck the adhesive to her own finger. "What else did you hear?"

"I'm not sure. The blood loss from these cuts is making me woozy. I should eat." He climbed out of the tub. "What did you bring me for breakfast?"

Mixing up the conversation, convincing her to smile and go along with his antics. How did he do that? "A Belgian waffle and lots of bacon."

"Define lots."

"Ginormous."

Scott grinned. "I'm feeling better already."

While he cleaned up, she warmed the food in the microwave.

Minutes later, Scott sat down in the adjoining dining room at the oval table where she'd set the plate on a blue place mat. "This looks great. Did you make it?"

"No. Belgian waffles are Ben's specialty, and no one, including me, gets in his way when it comes to making them. And this is nothing. For brunch on Sundays, he goes all out with flavors and toppings." She was rambling, but stopping would mean talking, and she wasn't quite ready for that. "Would you like some orange juice or I could make some coffee?"

"Orange juice is fine, but only if you're having a glass with me along with some of this." He pointed to the food.

Eating was actually a great way to stay occupied during the most embarrassing conversation on earth. Rina brought a saucer and utensils to the table along with two glasses of orange juice. She sat to his left at the head of the oval.

After giving in to her request for only a quarter of the waffle instead of half, he dug into his food. "Let's talk about the leak first."

As she took a sip from her glass, relief at not jumping into their other conversation mingled with a hint of anxiety about the fate of her tub. "What's the verdict?"

"If all goes well, I'll find the problem where it should be and fix it. After that the wall will have to stay open for a few days to dry out and make sure the repair is good. Do you have a dehumidifier?"

"I don't think so."

"I'll check and see if they have one at the hardware store. Actually, I better pick up two. We'll need one for the men's room."

We. That's what Dennis used to say whenever he'd talk about a repair. But Scott wasn't an employee with a vested interest in the form of a paycheck. "All this seems like a lot of work. You don't have to put in time doing it. I can call a plumber."

"With the set closed, all I have right now is time and I don't like sitting around doing nothing. Darby mentioned that you had a few odd jobs around the cafe that needed to be done. I can take care of them, too."

"That's too much to ask."

"Not if we're indulging in having fun together." He held up his hand stalling her objection. "All I'm saying is that if you'd like to share more waffles or ice cream or maybe even dinner with me sometime, I'd be willing to accept that in exchange for more work."

"That doesn't sound like a fair trade for all you're doing."

"You're right. Throw a few desserts my way, along with everything else, and we'll call it even." He lifted his glass of orange juice, ready to seal the agreement with a toast. "Sound like a deal?"

Two days later, Scott walked through the doors of Brewed Haven at the end of the lunch rush. He searched the dining area and the counter for Rina, but didn't see her. By the time he'd arrived at her apartment that morning, she'd already left. He'd sent a text letting her know he that he was there. She'd volleyed back texting him to let her know if he needed anything. Seeing her would have been nice, but the parameters of their new relationship didn't exactly require an in-person connection for it to work.

To friendship. That had been the toast Rina had made when she clinked her glass to his, and agreed to it. Holding her, kissing her, those things were off limits according to the definition. His handyman services in exchange for spending time together as friends and a few desserts. That wasn't what he wanted, but she did, and he wouldn't press her for more.

A server stopped by his table and he ordered a burger and fries. As he waited, Scott searched the internet for the next closest home improvement store. His father had reached out to check on him last night to see how he was progressing with the repair. He'd told his dad that he was having problems finding the parts he needed at the local hardware store along with dehumidifiers.

He'd also been truthful with his father about what was happening with *Shadow Valley*—that filming was still on hold, but there was a good chance they would start shooting around Nash soon, and he needed to remain available. Once again, his dad had smiled and said he understood about him not making it to the wedding. But now, he kept wondering if that were true. Was Wendy right about their dad being really disappointed that he wouldn't be there?

"Your burger, sir." Rina set the full plate on the table and flashed a cheerful smile as she slipped into the other side of the booth. "Make sure it's the way you like it."

He'd eat the burger, even if it was raw or tough as leather. Now that she was there, talking to him, he wasn't giving her a reason to get up and leave.

He took a bite and juicy perfection settled his growling stomach. "Medium well, just like I ordered."

"Good." She settled back in the seat. "So what's happening with the shower?"

As he poured catsup next to the fries, he noticed her staring at his plate. "Want some?"

"No. I'll eat later."

He took another bite of his burger. It would have been even better if she were sharing lunch with him. He'd enjoyed having breakfast with her the other morning. "The good news—I didn't see any mold inside the walls, and the hardware store in the next town has dehumidifiers. I'm picking them up today. That and the bathroom fan should dry up any moisture."

"And the bad news?"

Her brow furrowed. He hated to see her worried. If only he could just erase the problem overnight. "There's a mix of older metal and newer PVC pipes behind the wall. The metal ones in the area I cut away are corroded so I'll replace them. Honestly, I think I should check a wider section in the wall just in case more of them need to be switched out."

"So it's a much bigger job than expected?"

"It doesn't have to be. I can just replace the back-flow valve and the pipes attached to it."

Rina hesitated in reaching for a fry and sagged back in the seat. "But it's probably better to get it all done now. Like I should have in the first place when the contractor told me."

"Why didn't you?"

"At the time, down here, the plumbing was in ter-rible shape and had to be replaced. Upstairs, the situ-ation with the pipes wasn't ideal but good enough to pass a building inspection. I wanted to open in time for the Fourth of July. The only way I could make that date was by having the contractor install new plumbing down here but not upstairs."

"I could see where you'd make that decision. Fourth of July sales probably gave you a nice rev-enue bump."

"But it was a bad decision."

"I didn't say that."

"But Zurie did. She said my decision would come back and bite me and she was right." Rina reached toward the plate again but pulled back empty-handed.

Whatever this thing was between Rina and her sister caused Rina to waver between frustration and uncertainty. Maybe it wasn't his business, but it needed to stop. "I didn't realize Zurie owned Brewed Haven?"

Agitation flashed through Rina's expression. "She doesn't own the cafe. This place is mine."

"The way you're talking right now, it sure doesn't sound like it. Of course the contractor recommended you replace everything. Part of his job was to maximize the opportunities to make more money, and as the owner of Brewed Haven, that was your job, too. Being open for one of the biggest holidays of the year was a smart call, and from the looks of this place you, not Zurie, have been making the right decisions. Acknowledge that, stop second-guessing yourself and stop drooling over my fries. Eat some."

Rina stared back at him and blinked with a neutral expression.

Shit. Was it too soon in their friendship for blunt honesty?

Long seconds later, she slipped a fry from the pile on his plate. "Maybe you're right. And I wasn't drooling."

Relief hit him squarely in the chest. "If you weren't drooling over the fries, that means you were drooling over me."

"Seriously? Please tell me you're not that conceited."

"It's not conceit, just deductive reasoning. The only things in this booth beside you is the food and me. You just said you weren't drooling over my fries so that leaves only one option."

"You wish." Laughing, she flung a fry at him.

Even though he was momentarily caught off guard that she'd start a food fight, he caught it. Actually he did wish she wanted him. Then he wouldn't have to keep denying that he wanted her, too. Hell, maybe he should just tell her. And maybe she'd totally reject him. And then, there wouldn't be moments like this where he saw her happy and with her guard down.

He ate the fry she'd tossed at him. "Act nice. This isn't that type of an establishment. The boss will kick us out."

Smiling, she picked up another fry. "A trouble-maker like you, definitely. But I'm on good terms with management."

Chapter Fourteen

Rina studied the two pies on the kitchen prep table at Brewed Haven. The sweet smell of baked goods hung in the air along with near silence. Busy days at the cafe that week had kept her from testing new recipes. Toward the end of dinner that night, she'd finally gotten a few moments to make the pies. Now that the cafe was closed, it was the perfect time to analyze them.

The only staff hanging around late on a Saturday night was Darby, who was working on schedules. And Scott and his friend.

Booted footfalls in the rear storeroom and the rattle of a metal ladder signified their presence. The flickering storeroom light hadn't been just a simple bulb change but an issue with the fixture itself. He'd brought Owen, another member of the stunt crew, with him who was a trained electrician to help fix it.

The two's laughter traveled from the back of the kitchen. She easily picked out Scott's baritone chuckle, and her heart thumped with a beat that expanded in her chest. Since they'd shared fries in the booth almost two weeks ago, she'd had that experience every time they'd taken a moment for coffee, a meal in the cafe or an ice cream together by the fountain, or really whenever he was in proximity.

She'd also enjoyed their lighthearted conversations about random topics while he'd repaired the pipes. Athlete or nerd—they'd both been a little of each growing up. *Star Wars* or *Star Trek*—that debate remained unsettled. Introvert or extrovert. Almost always an extrovert for him. Conditional extrovert for her. Happy or grumpy morning person—after a hot shower or coffee he was good to go. Coffee was her preference later in the day. It took a cup of Positive Energy tea plus a long shower in silence to help her feel close to human first thing in the morning. Thanksgiving or Christmas—that was the only time they'd deviated into more serious territory as she'd shared how losing her parents had impacted her perception of the holidays. They didn't feel as joyful. Scott could relate when it came to his parents' divorce.

Social engagements between two people, most often involving food, and the two people are attracted to each other...

Sure she was attracted to Scott, but that didn't make Philippa's dating definition right. Plenty of friendships probably involved some level of attraction. Just because Scott ranked high on the eye candy meter or that she looked forward to their moments together more and more, didn't mean she had to act on any impulses those two things might inspire. She just had to keep her mind on the friendship part and what was important like nailing the contract with Gwen's Garden.

Rina focused back on the pies. Both were in a flaky crust and were filled with a custard that she hoped was the perfect blend of the three main ingredients: pecans, chocolate and a touch of alcohol. One had bourbon, the other rum.

Rina carried the pies out front and put them on the counter. "Would you mind giving me your opinion?"

Darby, working at a table by the window, mocked huge relief as she stood. "Bless you. I've been dying over here. They smell amazing."

"Hopefully they taste just as good." Rina walked behind the counter for rolled silverware and plates.

Having participated in tastings in the past with Rina, Darby went to the coffee station for two cups of water.

Once the pies were cut, they settled onto stools next to each other.

Rina pointed. "The slice on the left of your plate has rum in it. The one on the right has bourbon."

Darby took bites from one slice, cleansed her palate with water, then sampled the other.

Rina did the same. They tasted okay.

Darby pointed to the rum version on the left. "Definitely this one."

"Really?" Rina's pick leaned toward the one on the right. "Does it need something?"

"Chocolate. More is always better in my opinion. And maybe a skosh more rum, too." Darby licked the fork and winked. "You can't go wrong with more alcohol."

"Rum?" Scott walked out of the corridor into the dining room with Owen. "You guys are having a party and you didn't invite us?"

Owen grinned. "That's not right." Slightly shorter and stockier than Scott, his shaved head and a snub nose gave him the appearance of a brawler, but his smile was friendly.

"Consider yourself invited." Darby glanced at Owen and got up. "Take a seat and have some dessert. I've got to get going. I'm supposed to meet my girlfriends at the wine bar."

Scott leaned an elbow on the counter as he stood next to Rina.

The space around her seemed to shrink as the heat from his body radiated across the inches between them. She focused harder on Owen who was speaking to her.

"Mind if I take a rain check on dessert?"

"Of course. Anytime you want something. Just ask."

Owen glanced at Darby gathering her things at the table. He clapped Scott on the back. "You still need me?"

"Nope, I'm good. Thanks for the assist."

"No problem." Owen hurried after Darby who was walking out the door.

Scott's gaze landed on Rina. "I guess it's just the two of us."

"Yes. Just us." Rina stared at him.

Satisfaction ticked Scott's heart rate up a notch. Being alone with her was the best part of his day.

"So," Rina breathed out as she looked to the pies. "You're wondering about these, right? No, you're not. You already know what's going on."

Answering her own questions. She did that when she was nervous. Was she unsure about the pics or something else? "I'm guessing you're testing pecan pie recipes and from what I heard, they have rum in them?"

"They're actually chocolate pecan pies. The one on the left has rum. The other has bourbon. Want to try them?"

"Of course. I like getting paid." As Scott walked behind her, heading for the stool Darby had vacated, he quelled what felt like a natural urge to wrap his arms around her from behind. It was too easy for him to imagine her looking over her shoulder at him, and then kissing her.

"Great." Rina walked around to the other side of the counter, putting space between them. She took out a clean plate from below and put a slice of each pie on it. "Hold on. You need water." When she came back, as she reminded him what he needed to do for the tasting, her hands swept over the pies.

So many times over the past few days, he'd also wanted to reach across the table and hold her hand when they'd shared coffee or a meal or when they walked to the town square and sat by the fountain, but the constraints of their friendship held him back. He didn't want to lose what they had, but sometimes, not having the freedom to let her know how he truly felt about her was like trying to function on small sips of air when he needed to breathe.

Rina giving him a puzzled look brought him back to the present. "Don't forget to drink water in between sampling the two pies."

"Got it." He took bites from each pie. The nutty chocolate sweet flavor of the filling blended perfectly with the buttery pie crust. "They're both great. Which one do you like the most?"

"I don't know. Honestly, I'm not sure about anything anymore." She walked around the counter and stood beside him. "I've tried at least a half dozen different recipes for nut pies, fruit pies even cheesecake, but nothing stands out as special enough for a dessert line."

"It sounds like you need a diversion."

"I'm already distracted. That's my problem." Her arm brushed his as she unconsciously leaned on him a bit.

He shifted more toward her, pleased that she wasn't moving away. "A diversion isn't the same as a distraction. It's a change. In your case, doing something out of your wheelhouse might actually save you time by jumpstarting your ideas."

"Why do I get the feeling you really mean jumping off of something?"

"Now that you mention it, that might not be a bad idea."

"And end up like Nash?" She laughed. "I don't think so."

"Nash wasn't jumping off of anything. He stumbled and fell. Weren't you the one who said that when you fall, you learn how to face adversity by getting back up? But doesn't that lesson start with trying something first?" The urge to kiss away the small crumb of dessert on the corner of her mouth was so strong, Scott drank water to stop himself. "What do you have to lose by trying a diversion?"

She tilted her head and looked at him. "I can see it on your face. You've already thought of something. What is it?"

As the idea continued to take shape in his mind, Scott couldn't stop a smile. "It's a surprise. I promise it will be a good one. Don't ask questions. Just trust me."

Chapter Fifteen

The next morning, Rina parked in the lot at the stable. As she got out and shut the door, her gaze drifted to the barn in the middle of the pasture. Scott was expecting her to meet him in a few minutes.

What do you have to lose by trying a diversion?

That's what he'd said to her last night. When she'd pressed him about what he had in mind, he still wouldn't tell her. He'd just repeated, *Trust me.* And with those two little words, he'd circumvented the voice inside of her demanding caution. He'd given her only reasons to trust him from the first moment he'd shown up at the cafe so why say no? Especially when she needed to get past her creative block.

But even though she trusted him, she'd still stayed up half the night wondering. And remembering. Her first time riding on the back of a motorcycle. Feeling the rumble and purr of a powerful sports car through the steering wheel and opening up the engine on a vacant back road. Gambling with a seemingly endless stack of chips at a casino. Riding blindfolded on a rollercoaster. Xavier had given her those experiences. For him, every day had been about pushing past some invisible limit that only he could see. At first, it had been exciting, but later on, it had become frightening.

But Scott was different. Sure he took chances with his profession, but there was a solidness to him. He was dependable, and she felt safe with him. Even knowing that, walking across the pasture, knots of apprehension wound like knots inside of her. As she drew closer to the barn, Scott's and Owen's voices filtered out the door. She walked inside.

Both men stood near a metal scaffold off to the side near a rope hanging down that was connected to a cord. The cord ran up to the ceiling and ran along a beam to the middle of the barn.

Maybe they were working and she was interrupting?

Scott looked over at her and smiled. "You're here."

"Hi." She gave a small wave. "If you two are busy, I can wait."

"No. You're right on time," Scott said.

"Are you rehearsing a stunt?"

"No." Scott's gaze held Rina's as he approached her. "But we're going to do one. Or at least you are."

"Me? Perform a stunt? Wait. You don't want me to swing out of the barn like you did the day you ran me over?"

Owen chuckled.

Scott sent him a look. "Almost ran you over. But no. I'm going to teach you how to fly."

"Seriously?" The part of her that was intrigued outweighed the tiny voice inside of her saying no. "How?"

"I'll show you." He took her hand and gently pulled her to the center of the barn where a cord dropped down from the ceiling over an X marked in blue tape on the floor. "Have you ever seen a stage production of *Peter Pan*?"

"Not on stage but I did see the live show on television."

"One of the ways actors can fly through the air is with a rigging system. This one works by running a rigging wire through two fixed points. The pulley above where Owen is standing by the rope and then the one over our heads."

She let go of his hand and touched the thin black cord with a clip that was hanging down from the pulley above them. "Is this supposed to hold me?"

"I know it might not look like it but that wire is strong enough to support my weight. It will hold you up easily." He motioned to Owen who brought over what looked like a series of belts. "You'll be in this harness clipped to the wire. Owen is going to be over there by the scaffold pulling you up. I'll be right here teaching you what to do and spotting your every move. Do you want to try it?"

Nervous jitters intertwined with a healthy dose of excitement. In some ways, it was almost like riding a rollercoaster but not blindfolded. And he and Owen were both professionals. Safety and precautions were part of their job, not taking reckless chances. And this was a chance to fly like the free-spirited Peter Pan? How could she pass that up?

She looked to him and nodded. "Yes. I'll do it."

Owen took her keys and phone, and Scott helped her step into the harness that fit around and through her legs, around her back and across her chest. "Now I'm going to tighten this to a point that might feel a bit uncomfortable."

"Do what you have to do." He could make the harness more than a bit uncomfortable if it meant she wouldn't fall out of it.

Scott smoothing his hands over the straps raised tingles. By the time he finished, her knees felt a little weak.

Once she was secure, Scott attached the wire to the back of the harness.

Owen stood near the scaffold, gloves on, holding on to the end of the rope. He pulled and the wire grew taut, tugging her from the back and lifting her slightly before settling her back down.

"Whoa." She held her hands out to her sides as nerves loosed butterflies in her stomach.

Scott held her by the waist. "Relax. You're good. I've got you."

His gentle but firm hold alleviated doubts, but his closeness wreaked havoc on her concentration.

As if sensing her mind wanting to drift, he gave her a slight squeeze before letting go. His expression, more serious than she'd ever seen him, snapped her thinking into place. "Slouching will make the harness really uncomfortable. Pretend you're a ballet dancer. Head up, stand straight, engage your core."

Rina thought about her riding days. To stay straight in the saddle, she'd often pretended there was a string pulling her up from the top of her head.

"Good. Just like that. We're going to try a simple lift first. Owen's going to pull you straight up then set you down, nice and slow. When you land, don't lock your knees. Keep them soft." Scott demonstrated, jumping up from the ground and landing with his knees slightly bent.

Rina copied him.

"I think you're ready. Let's do it." He gave Owen a nod.

Using his body weight, Owen pulled down on the rope hand over hand.

As Rina lifted straight into the air, her breath whooshed out of her with a squeal of shock and delight.

"You alright up there?" Scott asked.

The harness cut into her inner thighs a little, but

the wonderful weightless feeling made up for it.
"Yes. I'm good."

"Try some small graceful movements. Lift your
hands to your sides. Up above your head. Good. Now
pretend like you're running in slow motion."

Rina did the latter, moving her arms and bicycling
her legs. She couldn't stop a giggle as she imagined
what she must look like running on air.

"Perfect," Scott said. "Let's try coming down."

Disappointment that she couldn't stay up there
made her slump, but the harness digging in reminded
her to straighten up. Rina descended for a soft but
wobbly landing. "Oh my gosh. Can we do it again?
That was fun."

Scott laughed. "You think that was fun?" He
pointed her to a corner in the barn. "You're going
to start over there. When you're lifted up, lean your
body toward home. That's the X."

What was going to happen dawned on her. This
was the flying part! Rina went to the corner and
faced the X. "I'm ready."

She was lifted up, and Rina leaned in as she flew
back toward center. "Woooo!" She landed and when
Owen lifted her back up, she soared back to the corner.

Again and again, she moved to the different starting places Scott indicated and flew through the air.

Owen had to leave and Scott took over.

As she kept flying, all of her cares and worries

about the cafe and what was or wasn't coming in the future magically slipped away.

As Scott pulled down on the rope, the muscles in his arms and legs began to burn from repetition, but he endured it, mesmerized by the expression of bliss on Rina's face as she flew through the air, her braids flowing behind her.

She laughed and the pure rich sound filled him with happiness…and a bit of sadness that this moment would come to an end. It was beautiful. She was beautiful…a force in her own right. Sometimes, he got the feeling she didn't know how truly amazing she was.

He lowered her slowly over the X.

Firmly on the ground, Rina leaned over from the waist and massaged her thighs. The tight straps were starting to take a toll on her.

"Stay there. I'll disconnect you." He secured the rope to the scaffold before walking over to her.

Scott detached her and helped her loosen the harness. When there was enough slack in the straps, she slipped the harness from her shoulders and pushed it past her hips to her feet.

"That was amazing." She rubbed the sides of her ribcage and winced.

Concern made him drop the harness and lay his hands below hers on her waist. "I kept you up there too long." Shit. He knew better than that. "Does it hurt when you breathe? How bad is it?"

"I'm fine. That experience was totally worth the pain."

He'd rather have skipped that last part for her. "You really enjoyed it?"

"You know I did." Rina looked up at him. "Thank you. This was exactly what I needed." Seconds passed as she didn't step back and he didn't let her go. Then she moved a little closer.

Friendship. That's what Rina wanted, and he respected that. But being near her like this chipped away at his resolve. The voice in his head telling him to let go was lost in the sound of his heart beating faster and echoing inside of him.

Rina laid her hands on his chest.

He leaned in a fraction, waiting and hoping she wouldn't push him way. Scott lowered his mouth to hers and as soon as she opened to him, arousal flared. The control he'd held on to so closely around her for too many long weeks, days and hours weakened to nothing. Rina slid her arms around his neck and he wrapped his arms firmly around her. Every stroke and glide of their deepening kiss driving him nearer to pure want.

She pressed closer and her breasts pillowing against his chest short-circuited his brain to just one thought. *More*. Taking hold of her hips, he brought her against him, letting her feel how much he wanted her. But now wasn't the time. Still he stroked his hands upward, gliding them under the hem of her shirt. The warmth of her skin seeped into him. He desperately wanted to kiss her there and any place the straps of the harness may have left a temporary mark or a bruise.

Rina eased back from the kiss.

He drew in an unsteady breath and stared into her eyes. "Just so you know, I'm not sorry that happened."

"Neither am I."

"So does that mean we might get to do that again outside of the barn?"

Her gaze dropped as she slid her hands to his chest. His hopes sank in the silence. Had that kiss cost him everything?

She looked back up at him and smiled. "There's more than a possibility that could happen again."

They were officially out of the friend zone and moving into new territory. *Finally.* If only he didn't have to meet Kyle and the rest of the stunt crew. They'd just gotten the word that morning about the new schedule. For the rest of the upcoming week, he and the other stunt performers were rehearsing stunts. The week after that, filming around Nash would take place.

He briefly pressed his lips to hers. "I'm tied up until late this afternoon. What about you?"

"I took the day off. I'm trying out recipes in my apartment."

"Is it okay if I drop by later to put up the drywall?"

"Sure. I'll make us dinner."

Did that soft look in her eyes mean that dinner

included more kisses? If he had a say in it, kissing her would be a part of the appetizers, main course and dessert. But right then… "I have to get going."

She took her arms away. "I should get going, too."

"Give me a minute to take care of a few things, and I'll walk you to your car."

After giving Rina her keys and phone, he locked the harness in a storage trunk near the scaffold and secured the rope and wire. Outside, he padlocked the barn. As they started walking toward the parking lot, Scott took her hand and intertwined their fingers. He was going to hold her hand every chance he got.

Chapter Sixteen

As Rina walked across the pasture with Scott it felt like she was still flying on air. Kissing him hadn't been part of the plan, it had just happened. And like she'd told him, she wasn't sorry about it. But what it meant for them going forward, she didn't know. He was around for only a short time and—*Stop*. She was overcomplicating things before they'd even gotten a chance to talk about what was going on between them.

Beside her SUV, she faced him and stepped into his loose embrace. "See you later."

"Can't wait."

Scott kissed her and she wrapped her arms around him. Whatever this was, she liked the holding and kissing part...a lot.

Tires crunched on rocks in the parking lot.

In her periphery, she saw the dark SUV pull in two spaces down. *Tristan.*

In a knee-jerk reaction, she took her arms from around Scott and ended the kiss.

A puzzled expression came over his face. He glanced that direction, but didn't let her go.

Not that he needed to—she was a grown woman and had every right to be with Scott. But this was the first time in years that she'd put her personal life on blast.

Chloe Daniels opened the front passenger door and got out. Her rose-colored blouse, skinny jeans and high-heeled sandals were casual, but from the color and contours of the makeup highlighting her light brown face, she'd just come from the set.

Tristan, walking around the rear of the vehicle from the driver side, also appeared to be off the clock. He had on a pair of clean jeans and instead of a navy shirt with the embroidered Tillbridge logo— a white horse and *T* with a lasso around it—he had on a white short-sleeved pullover.

Chloe smoothed a strand of long dark wavy hair from her eyes and waved enthusiastically. Her smile was infectious.

"Hi." Genuinely happy to see her, Rina slipped from Scott's arms to greet Chloe and share a big hug. They hadn't seen much of each other since the welcome buffet for the cast and crew almost three weeks ago, and even then, she hadn't gotten a chance to really talk to her. "It's so good to see you."

"You, too." Chloe squeezed back. As she let go, she glanced over Rina's shoulder. "Hi, Scott."

"Hi, Chloe." As he walked over to them, Tristan did, too.

The two men said "Hey" to each other and exchanged a firm handshake that seemed a tad long.

"What are you guys doing here?" Rina asked.

"I'm finished for the day," Chloe replied. "We just stopped by so Tristan could grab something from his office and then we're going to the house. What about you two?" As she looked between Rina and Scott with open curiosity, Tristan slipped an arm around her waist.

Scott's arm brushed Rina's as he moved closer, not to stake a claim, but as if to let her know he was there for her.

Rina pointed to him. "Scott was showing me the rigging they use to simulate flying in the air."

Tristan's brow raised a fraction.

Chloe's face animated with interest. "Really? Did you try it?"

"Yes." Rina looked to Scott and shared a smile with him. "I could have stayed up there all day long, but I've got things to do and he does, too."

"I wish you didn't have to go." Chloe frowned in disappointment. "We haven't talked in forever. We really have to make time to catch up with each other."

"No time like the present." Tristan glanced from Rina to Scott. "What are you two doing later today?"

Rina took two casual dresses from her closet and tossed them on the bed. Blue and blue. When had her wardrobe become so boring? What had possessed Scott to say yes?

When Tristan had mentioned joining him and Chloe for an early dinner, she'd been ready to back up Scott's no, but instead he'd asked what time they should show up and should they bring anything. And just like that, their quiet night alone figuring out where they were headed in their new relationship was going had leapfrogged to date night. Philippa would cry with laughter when she told her, but there was nothing humorous about the situation. Scott and Tristan's gripping handshake and that eye-to-eye stare. What was going on with them?

Rina chose the floral midi dress on the left with thin shoulder straps and got dressed. After almost putting her eye out with the mascara wand and blotting off more of her berry lipstick, she slipped on a pair of cute wedge heel sandals, grabbed her purse, and left.

She arrived ten minutes early to pick up Scott at the guesthouse. Instead of waiting for him to come down, she tucked her purse underneath the seat, locked the car, and went up to the second floor.

A short time after she knocked, he answered. Faded jeans encased his long legs and he wore high-tops instead of boots. His untucked pale-blue button-down shirt with sleeves rolled up near his elbows made his eyes more blue than green.

"Hey." Scott motioned her inside. "I just need to grab my wallet and my phone. Am I late? I must have lost track of time." He walked to the dresser.

The clean smell of soap and his cologne hung in the remnants of steam from the corner bathroom. That, his slicked back damp hair, and the white towel lying on the navy comforter filled her mind with images of him in the shower. It took more than one mental shake to make them go away.

Rina walked further into the room. "No you're not late. I'm early. I thought we should talk."

His phone chimed and he snagged it from the dresser. As Scott stared at the screen, he frowned. "About what?"

"This cookout with Tristan and Chloe. You don't have to go. I know you might feel obligated."

His head snapped up from his phone. "Obligated?" Scott set down the phone and walked over to her. Just as she went to explain what she meant, he cupped her cheek and captured her mouth. He took his time exploring, teasing, chasing until her knees grew weak.

Scott pulled back and looked into her eyes. "Did that feel like obligation to you?"

"No." It took effort for her not to lean in for another kiss. "But still, I need you to know you don't have to do this just because Tristan was acting over-protective."

"I'm not doing this for him. I'm doing this for us." He led her to the dresser, leaned back against it, and drew her between his legs. "You and Tristan are close. Things need to be good between the three of us if you and I are going to enjoy the time we have together. And as far as him being protective, I get it. If I'd driven up on some guy I only knew in passing kissing my sister, I'd want to get a read on him, too."

"And your sister? If she were here, would she go out of her way to pull me aside to get a read on me?"

"Wendy?" A chuckle shot out of him. "Hell yeah. I'd probably have to stop her from running your fingerprints for a background check." He kissed the back of her hand. "It's a good thing that he cares about you so much and wants to know what's going on."

That was a good question that they should probably clear up before going to Tristan's. "Us spending time together. What does that mean now that we're a little more than friends?"

"What more means is up to you. I'm just glad that I get to kiss you. It was tough holding back."

He held her by the waist and she rested her hands on his shoulders. "Why did you?"

"Because you wanted to be strictly friends and I was respecting that."

The sincerity in his eyes made her heart swell and stir desire. It was so darn easy to want more with him, maybe too easy, and that part battled inside of her. But his ask was straightforward—let's spend time together. She'd complained about the drama in relationships. Maybe this time, she was taking something simple and making it more dramatic than it needed to be. And doing that was also a huge distraction. She liked Scott, a lot, and it was more of a disruption in her life to keep denying it.

Rina took a step closer and her thighs brushed against his. "While you're here, I want us to be able to enjoy being together. No holding back."

"I like the sound of that." His gaze moved down to her wedge heels and back up to her face. "I should have said this when you first walked in. You look beautiful."

The same level of desire simmering inside of her was in his eyes. "Thank you."

Just as they started to lean toward each other, his phone chimed. As he glanced down at the text bubble on the screen, his expression grew a tad irritated. Instead of taking a moment to respond, he snatched it up along with his wallet. "We should get going."

Outside in her SUV, he sat in the front as a passenger and she drove.

Along the four-lane road, houses were interspersed with cows and horses grazing in pastures and farmland.

Scott stared out the side window. "How far away is Tristan's place?"

"Not far. About twenty miles."

"That's not a bad commute, living out here. In LA, twenty miles would be a totally different story."

"True, but Tristan doesn't always commute. He splits time between here and his cottage on the property. When he's working late or has an early morning meeting, it's easier for him to stay there instead of driving home." Rina moved to the left lane, accelerated past a couple cars and glided back in. "But if Chloe starts spending more time in Maryland, I'm sure he'll adjust his hours and spend more time with her out here."

"This is a nice area." Scott settled back in the seat. "Didn't I read somewhere that your family home used to be on the property?"

"Yes. It was right where the guesthouse is now."

"Was it hard to see it torn down?"

The question wasn't reflective of what had become their usual lighthearted banter, but it was a legitimate one. The image of the large two-story home that had once existed came into her mind. By the time she'd moved out six years ago, both her parents were gone and Tristan was still in the army. The house was no longer the vibrant welcoming space where she, Zurie and Tristan had grown up. Every room, corner and tiny space was just a shell, void of the happiness they'd once shared as a family, and highlighting all they'd lost.

"No. It was time to move on." Rina glanced at Scott. "Where did you and Wendy grow up?"

"A few places. Before my parents divorced, we

lived in New Jersey—a nice house in a middle-class neighborhood. After they split up, my mom moved closer to her family in Connecticut. My dad eventually moved to North Carolina with his new wife. After that he moved every time he got married, Georgia, then where he is now in Florida." He huffed a chuckle. "But that could change now that he's marrying again. I think she's from Maine or maybe Vermont."

His dad had been married four times and was about to make it five? Was her math right? That was interesting. "Is the wedding soon?"

"Very soon." Scott's expression remained impassive.

Curiosity needled her but he didn't elaborate. "Did your mom remarry?"

"No. She's happy at her dream job. She's a curator for a museum."

A short time later, Rina turned onto a gravel road that joined with a long paved one. It cut through an expansive area of neatly clipped grass bordered with trees and ended at modern two-story with a double-pitched roof, beige brick, blue siding and white trim.

She pulled to the side of the house and parked on the left outside of the two-car garage.

They got out and Scott let her precede him as they walked down the light stone path to the front porch.

A small bit of jitters went through her as she rang the doorbell. This was her first time socializing with Tristan in a couple's situation.

Scott laid his hand on her lower back and gave her a wink.

Chloe opened the door and greeted them with a huge smile. The heavy makeup was gone and she'd changed into a casual peach sundress. "Come in." She stepped back and let them inside. "Tristan had to run to the store. He should be back soon."

The last time Rina had been in Tristan's place it was mostly empty. As Rina walked inside with Scott, an exclamation of surprise slipped out as she took in the updated cream-walled dark-wood space. "Oh, this is lovely. Did you do all of this?"

Chloe smiled as she shut the door behind them. "I added a few touches here and there, but Tristan's been involved with every decision. This is his house. I'll give you the grand tour." She pointed left. "Tristan decided to turn this into a sitting room instead of a formal dining space."

An overstuffed oat-colored couch with colorful paisley pillows sat against the wall facing the window overlooking the porch and the front lawn. Potted rubber tree plants in brass pots and glass-topped furniture were the perfect unobtrusive accents.

"We also made a few changes in here, too." Chloe led them forward past the beige carpeted steps to the expansive open living room with high ceilings.

It was embraced by light coming in through the windows in the front and the large sliding door and windows on the opposite side. A patterned rug, oatmeal-colored side chairs and a dark-wood coffee table complemented the sapphire-blue couch that Rina recognized.

"A few changes?" Rina huffed a laugh. "These are major. It's no longer a guy cave with just a couch and a flat screen television."

Scott chuckled. "And the problem with that was?"

Chloe's laugh and expression reflected exactly what was in Rina's mind. *Typical guy.*

"Wall art is the next on the list of things to buy." Chloe's cell phone rang on the coffee table and she picked it up. "It's my agent. I need to take this, but keep exploring, and definitely check out the office."

Rina led the way down a small hallway to the right of the stairs into what had once been an empty room. Now it was a true working space. A wood desk and a comfortable-looking black leather desk chair faced a window, but the most striking additions were the three large picture boxes containing photos hanging on the wall behind the desk.

Scott walked behind the desk chair to get a closer look at the one on the left. "Is this you?"

She joined him, staring up at a collage of pictures of her younger self, dressed in English riding gear with her horse. Noble Wind.

Many of the pictures showed her and the gelding with white above its hooves and a star shape on its forehead soaring over fences in a competition. Others showed her standing next to him. One was of her at seventeen smiling with an arm affectionately wrapped around his neck as she held a first place prize ribbon. That was the start of a winning streak. One that hadn't changed her life as expected.

As she reached up and stroked near the photo of her and Noble Wind, sadness swelled in her chest. She looked away from it to the middle picture box. That one was filled with photos from Tristan's bull riding days. In the center of it was a belt buckle she recognized. Tristan and his father had won it in a team calf roping competition over a decade ago. It was the first time they'd ever done anything like that.

The far box on the right showed Zurie barrel racing. She'd been such a superstar back then.

All three of them had experienced some level of success in competitions, but then life had thrown them a curve. Her and Zurie's mother lost her life in a car accident. When their father inexplicably passed away in his sleep years later, many believed he'd died of a broken heart because not having his childhood sweetheart by his side was too much for him to take.

More emotions—sad but also loving—welled inside of Rina. In between losing her parents, she'd been in the accident with Xavier. That period of losing her mom, being in her own accident, then having her father pass away had been the decade from hell.

As if sensing an explanation of the photos was too much for her to share right then, Scott stood with her in companionable silence.

Movement at the door drew their attention.

As Tristan walked in, he nodded to Scott then looked to Rina. "What do you think?"

Swallowing past the slight lump in her throat, she smiled. "These are amazing."

"They were in my father's memorabilia collection." Tristan's gaze met hers and she saw what he wasn't saying aloud. His father's second wife had almost made off with the collection that had not only contained priceless family mementos but valuable ones, too.

Scott glanced at the blank wall. "What's going over there?"

"Lots of new memories, I hope." Tristan's gaze shifted to Chloe standing in the doorway, and they exchanged soft loving smiles. He shifted his attention to Scott. "So has Rina showed you her collection, yet?"

"Collection?" Scott looked down at Rina. "Where's your stuff hanging up at?"

"Hanging?" Tristan barked a chuckle. "She's got a stack of scrap and photo albums that are probably taller than she is."

Chloe giggled. "But don't worry, she'll break you in by showing you only four or five of them like she did with me."

"Hey," Rina interjected unable to stop a smile. "I only brought out three of them *and* I served you cocktails."

"True." Chloe laughed. "Speaking of cocktails, we should have some."

Chapter Seventeen

Close to an hour later, the four of them sat at the round patio table under an umbrella in the middle of the back deck that extended along the sides of the house.

The stunning view of acres of land in the back that included a small horse arena and small stable added to the relaxed atmosphere. Conversation flowed freely while they ate chicken kabobs, steak and salad.

Chloe and Scott traded experiences working on movie sets—they both agreed *Shadow Valley*'s director, Holland Ainsley, set the tone for a professional environment they appreciated.

Tristan asked Scott how he became a stuntman, and that segued into both of them sharing about their time in the military, as well as a little trash talk about army versus navy football. After some prompting, Scott had fessed up about which shows and movies he'd worked on in the past, many of which Chloe, Rina and Tristan were familiar with or had watched.

Rina answered Chloe's questions about how things were at the cafe. She didn't mention the Gwen's Garden contract, and if Tristan knew about the loan issue, he didn't let on. The topic of Scott helping her out with repairs came up. Upon discovering Scott's plumbing knowledge, Tristan asked for advice on a minor issue he was having with the hot tub on the corner of the deck.

During a lull in the banter, Chloe nudged Tristan. "We forgot dessert."

"Darn it," Rina said. "I meant to bring something from the cafe." But she'd been so preoccupied with wanting to talk to Scott before they came to dinner, it had completely slipped her mind.

Scott reached over and gave her hand a squeeze. "Is there a place nearby? I'll make a run if you tell me where to go."

"No." Chloe waved away the offer. "You're our guest. Relax."

A pie recipe Rina had tested that morning after her Peter Pan experience in the barn sparked inspiration. "What about the fresh berries I saw in the fridge? I could make something with that."

"Are you sure you don't mind?" Chloe asked. "You're our guest, too."

Rina stood. "Don't worry about it. Show me what you've got."

Inside the beige-countered kitchen, Chloe opened the fridge and gave her the two small containers that were inside of it—one with blackberries, the other with raspberries. "Oh wait. I think we have sugar cookie dough. We could just bake those."

"Or I can make something with the cookies and the berries." Rina peeked over Chloe's shoulder. "And that carton of heavy cream on the top shelf. What about the blackberry wine you mentioned picking up at the winery. Can I use some of that, too?"

"Sure. I'll open a bottle." Chloe grinned. "If you're adding that to it, whatever you're making will have to be good."

"We'll see."

After Chloe opened the wine, they worked together, baking the frozen sugar cookies and whipping the heavy cream.

As they waited for the cookies to bake, Rina peeked out the small window in the kitchen.

Tristan and Scott had taken care of clearing the table and were now walking toward the arena. They were deep in conversation. What were they talking about?

Chloe joined Rina. "I'm glad you two came over. I've seen Scott around but I haven't gotten a chance to really talk to him until today. I like him."

"Be sure to tell that to Tristan."

"Why? They seem to be getting along."

"I guess. Tristan was acting weird this morning when we ran into the two of you at the stable."

Chloe chuckled. "Yeah, he was kind of shocked to see you and Scott kissing in the parking lot. So how serious is it?"

"We're still figuring things out which is why I don't need Tristan feeling he has to be protective of me."

Chloe waved away her concern. "It's a guy thing. If it's any consolation, my brother was the same with him."

"Seriously? What happened?"

"They went outside and had a private conversation in the backyard. Just like you're doing now, I watched from the window. When it ended, they did the whole nod, clap on the shoulder ritual."

As if on cue, Tristan and Scott clapped each other on the back and clinked the top of their beer bottles together.

Chloe snorted a laugh. "See? I was close. Guy thing."

"Did Tristan tell you what your brother told him?"

"Are you kidding? And risk losing his man card? Guys have their own version of the sister solidarity code." Chloe nudged Rina's shoulder with hers. "Don't worry about their conversation. I know the way Tristan is acting feels archaic, but I'm sure Scott will take whatever he's saying for what it means—Tristan cares about you."

"I know." Rina went with Chloe to check the cookies.

It was just strange to see Tristan act this way about a guy she was seeing. He'd never been around to play that role in her life.

As Rina prepared dessert and Chloe washed dishes, a realization crept in. This place was no longer just a house but a home. And possibly a fresh start and a continuation of their family's legacy.

A daydream formed in Rina's mind. More couples' dinners. Having long chats with Chloe in the front sitting room. Holiday get-togethers, including a family tree trimming at Christmas. All of the wonderful moments they'd stopped celebrating fully, years ago, after too much tragedy had taken hold in their lives. But it was too soon to dream about that. Tristan and Chloe were serious about each other, but not engaged. And she and Scott had just acknowledged they wanted more than a basic friendship. And as far as she knew, Zurie wasn't even seeing anyone.

The sliding door opened and shut in the living room. A short time later, Tristan and Scott strolled into the kitchen.

"It smells good in here," Tristan boomed out. "And it looks even better." Smiling, he went over to Chloe at the sink. As she glanced over her shoulder, he kissed her.

Scott joined Rina at the counter by the stove. He didn't appear to be ticked off or intimidated by whatever Tristan had said to him. That was a good sign.

As he curved his hand into her waist, Scott kissed her temple and murmured. "He's right about the view."

A short time later, Rina doled out the impromptu dessert: sugar cookies nestled in a bowl with berries flavored with the blackberry wine, topped with cookie crumbs and whipped cream. They took them to the living room, where Chloe and Rina chose a rom-com flick that the guys mildly grumbled about having to watch. Afterward, Rina and Scott decided to head home.

In the driveway, Chloe and Scott walked ahead to the SUV, talking about Nash and changes to the shooting schedule.

Tristan wrapped an arm around Rina's shoulder, slowing their pace as he walked beside her. "So you and Scott are going to be seeing a lot of each other?"

"I don't know." She wrapped an arm around his waist. "What did Scott say when you threatened him into telling you his intentions?"

"Our conversation wasn't that deep, but I'm sure he knows I have an expectation about how I'd like him to treat you."

"Wow, thanks Dad. Can I please stay out an hour after curfew?"

"Nope." He grinned. "I still expect you home by ten."

Rina playfully poked him in the ribs. "In answer to your first question, Scott and I started out as friends and we've just recently decided to become more than that. Mainly, we just want to enjoy spending time together while he's here."

"Well, whatever spending time together means, and please don't elaborate, can I make a suggestion?"

"What?"

He slowed their pace even more. "Be honest about you and Xavier up front. You might not think telling him is relevant, but it is, especially for you."

She halted and faced him. "Why? Because I was injured in the accident?"

"No. Because Xavier broke your trust, and you haven't let a guy into your life until now with Scott. It's a big deal, and I think Scott needs to know that so he can act accordingly and you can, too."

Act accordingly? Irritation sparked in Rina. "You mean reevaluate whether or not I can handle us being more than just friends. I'm not a fragile piece of glass."

"I didn't say that. But a short-term thing, no strings attached, I just can't see you doing that."

Tristan may have been intervening from a caring place, but he didn't know what she could handle. Rina softened her tone but not her conviction. "I know you feel you have to worry about me, but don't. I can handle my personal life. I'll be with who I want for as long as it's right and right now, I'm happy with Scott."

Chapter Eighteen

On the way back to Tillbridge, Scott drove and Rina sat in the front passenger seat.

When he and Tristan had walked off the deck while Rina and Chloe were making dessert in the kitchen, he'd already anticipated what Tristan wanted to talk about.

So you and Rina are seeing each other? Tristan had asked.

Yes. And if you're worried about her, you don't have to be.

I'm not worried, Tristan had said, looking out over the yard before meeting him eye to eye. *I'm sure she wouldn't get involved with anyone who thought they could take advantage of her.*

I know where you're coming from. I have a

*younger sister. I'd want anyone she was with to treat
her with respect, too.*

After reaching that understanding, the conversation had switched to horses. The horse trainer for the movie had talked to Tristan about Showdown, one of the horses brought in for the production. He was the horse Nash and Scott were supposed to ride during filming and was the one that had wandered from his mark the day Nash had gotten injured. For some reason, Showdown had decided he no longer wanted to perform.

Rina reached over and laid her hand on his thigh. "Thanks again for agreeing to dinner."

"No need to thank me. I enjoyed it."

"Even after Tristan decided to grill you about our relationship."

Chuckling, he intertwined their fingers and kissed the back of her hand. "We came to a mutual understanding." Rina and Tristan talking just before they left flashed in his mind. "What about the two of you? The conversation you were having in the driveway before we left seemed kind of serious."

"Maybe a little." She slipped her hand from his to adjust the cross belt near her shoulder then stared out the front windshield.

Their conversation faded to silence. Rina turned on the radio and pop music filled the void.

She was preoccupied. Was it something that Tristan had said? Maybe he'd misread the situation, and Tristan did have a problem with him and Chloe being together.

By the next mile, the debate to ask her whether or not there was an issue had concluded in Scott's mind. He was letting it go. Rina knew where he stood about wanting to be with her. If something Tristan had said changed her mind, he'd be disappointed, but he'd meant it when he'd said that whatever happened outside of them being friends was up to her.

She switched off the radio. "Tristan said I should talk to you."

"About?"

"My past."

The tone of her voice and a quick glance at her face revealed a lot. "You don't have to tell me."

"No, he's right. I do." She looked straight ahead during the pause. "After I lost my mom, it was hard to see my future. My father bought Noble Wind and encouraged me to get serious about competing again."

"Was that the horse in the photo with you in Tristan's office?"

"Yes. From the start we were a good fit for each other. Right away, we started winning competitions. My trainer at the time felt we had a chance of making the US equestrian team."

"That says a lot. You must have been really good."

"We were, but we didn't make the team."

Farther up, the one-lane road opened up and he

shifted into the right lane. "That must have been tough for you."

"It was, and I had a hard time handling it." She stared out the windshield as if looking into the past. "I started partying a lot."

Scott set the cruise control at a moderate speed. Rina had something important to say and he wanted to listen.

"That's how I met Xavier. He raced street cars as a hobby and liked to bet on anything that moved. His father was co-owner of a casino in Vegas so money and access wasn't a problem for him. Being with him was new and exciting because his life was so different from mine."

He tried to imagine a younger Rina running reckless with a bad boy. He couldn't. The Rina he knew was so careful with her decisions, maybe overly cautious at times. "How did your family take it?"

"Not well. My dad and uncle urged me to stay away from him, but that was all they could do. I was eighteen and legally an adult. Tristan was serving in the army and had his own concerns. From Zurie's point of view, I was just being an irresponsible brat."

"So what happened?"

"I married him."

Chapter Nineteen

Rina paused to let Scott digest that bit of news as she took in how it felt to tell him. She hadn't planned on doing it. Tristan's reasoning didn't line up with hers, it made sense for a different reason.

As her friend, she had let Scott in further than most, sharing her fears about the cafe and her struggles with Zurie. Now that they'd agreed to be more than just friends, sharing the hardest moment of her life felt less like a big reveal and more of a natural progression. And besides that, when it came time for her and Scott to become intimate, he'd see her leg and wonder how it happened.

Scott glanced over at her. "You eloped?"

"Not exactly. One morning, before everyone woke up, a transport service Xavier had arranged picked up Noble Wind and a few hours later, we were on the road. I called home to let everyone know I was okay. A few days after that, when we arrived in Vegas, we were married at a 24-hour chapel."

With this ring, I thee wed... for richer or poorer... in sickness and in health...

When she'd made those vows to Xavier, she couldn't have imagined what was ahead for them.

Memories filtered through her mind, but they seemed distant, as if belonging to someone else. "At first, living one big party and having no responsibilities was fun, but after a few months, it grew tiresome. The cars, the condo, the furnishings inside of it, they didn't belong to us. Everything was in his father's name. We lived off of an allowance he gave us. We were supposed to make a life together, but we couldn't. I needed some sort of independence so I got a job teaching horse riding at the stable where we were boarding Noble Wind. That's also when I started baking pies. It reminded me of home."

"How much of this did your family know?"

"None of it. I thought I could change him. And I was too proud to admit I'd made a mistake."

"How long did you stay?" His low tone didn't hold judgment or accusation. It was a fair question.

"Eight months. By then, his gambling had grown out of control. He'd started going to private poker games with high stakes. What I could save from the allowance his father gave us, after he paid his debts, plus teaching horse riding and selling pies barely kept the lights on and food on the table."

Tillbridge just up ahead in the dusky sunset forced a pause.

Scott parked and turned off the engine. He unclipped his belt and turned toward her in the seat.

His silence was her cue to finish, but now that they were standing still, and she could see his face, telling him the rest, the hardest part, felt even harder.

Stalling, she unbuckled her seat belt as a memory more vivid than the others started to surface. "I decided to leave him. I'd gotten myself into the situation on my own. I thought I could get myself out of it. I just needed enough money to transport Noble Wind. One morning, I walked out of the condo and my car was gone. I didn't bother calling the police. I already knew why it was missing. But I hadn't expected to get to work and find Noble Wind was gone, too. Xavier had sold him and the car to pay off a debt."

Scott reached over the console and held her hand. "Do you know who bought him?"

"No. Later that day before the accident, Xavier showed up at the stable. All he'd said was that Noble Wind was safe. That the person who'd bought him owned horses." Rina swallowed past the tightness in her throat, willing herself to get through the rest. "That's the last conversation I remember. Days later, I woke up in the hospital. We'd been in a car accident… Xavier was already gone."

Scott's hand closed tightly around hers but he sat in the silence with her as she confronted the gaping hole that still existed in her memories. For months after the accident, she used to silently scream into the void, but all that would echo back was the pain of her injuries and the same accusation. If she hadn't gone away with Xavier, none of it would have happened. And she would still have Noble Wind.

As soon as she'd been well enough after the accident, she'd tried to get back on a horse, but it wasn't the same. She missed the bond she shared with Noble Wind so much she'd stopped riding.

Tears that wouldn't fall stung in her eyes.

The front passenger side door opened and Scott stood there. When had he gotten out of the driver's seat? He held out his hand.

She took it and as soon as she got out, he enfolded her in his arms.

Scott's long exhale blew over her temple as he tightened his hold. Solid strength seeped into her. "Thank you for telling me."

Rina held her breath, waiting, but he didn't say it. Scott hadn't said the word she'd forced herself to nod or smile through even though it felt like a dagger in her heart. Sorry for your loss. Sorry this happened to you. Sorry, we have to operate on your leg again. Sorry, the funeral already happened. Sorry, Xavier's family doesn't wish to speak with you. *Sorry...*

She looked up into Scott's unwavering gaze and tears escaped from her eyes. In the short time they'd known each other, he always knew what she needed to hear and how to show up for her. Even now, as she looked in his eyes, she could see that he knew.

Scott covered her mouth with his and the loss of the past started to recede in the firm pressure of his lips. The way he boldly swept in when she opened to him conveyed what she needed to feel. Alive. And what she strived so hard to be. Authentic in who she was now and not governed by her past.

She'd confronted her worst memory, and for the first time, she felt as if she hadn't looked into the void alone. Scott had done it with her and he wasn't shying away or treating her differently. What they felt for each other hadn't changed.

As Scott eased back, he stroked her cheek, searching her eyes.

Rina already knew the answer to the question in his. She was absolutely sure what she wanted. To let go and focus on now. She just wanted to enjoy being with him.

Upstairs in his room, Scott shut the door behind them.

She turned away from him to put her purse and phone on the end of the dresser and slip off her sandals.

His high-tops thunked to the floor, and soon after, Scott came up behind her. As he dropped his wallet and phone next to her things, he curved his hand into her waist. As he trailed kisses down the side of her neck, she tilted her head to give him better access. Leaning into him, she trembled with anticipation.

He retraced the path of his kisses back up to speak softly into her ear. "We'll go as fast or as slow as you want. We have all night."

His promise and Scott gliding his hands up her ribcage to cup her breasts pulled a shaky breath from her. His light feathering touch over her nipples created a longing that made her knees weak. She reached back and swept her ponytail forward over her shoulder, and Scott took his cue to unzip her dress. He took his time, kissing and caressing her shoulders and back as he slid down the straps and helped her shimmy out of it.

As she stood, still facing away from him in her silky beige strapless bra and lace boy shorts, a tiny voice of doubt crept in. What would he notice first? Her or the permanent reminder of what her past had left behind?

Rina turned in his arms. As his gaze swept down and up again, his jawline angled with a look of need that incinerated questions…and hesitation. She unbuttoned his shirt, mesmerized and excited by the reveal of tanned skin. As he took it off, the taut muscles in his torso naturally rippled. Drawn to him, she caressed his hard chest. As she moved down his abs he drew in a shaky breath. They became even more defined as she unfastened his jeans and unzipped him. He pushed them down to the floor and kicked them away. The evidence of his need rising behind his boxer briefs sent desire spiraling to her core. She glided her hands up his chest and around his neck and he brought her flush against him for a heated kiss. Feverish strokes and glides fueled caresses that pushed away lace, satin and cloth.

They fell onto the bed together, and soon she was lost in first touches and first kisses that made her ache. He raised soft emotions inside of her as he swept his lips over her right knee and up her thigh, following the trail of what the worse day in her life had left behind, only to take her to a place of ecstasy that had her chanting his name. Soon after Scott put on a condom, and as he entered her his eyes never left hers.

They moved as one. And found pleasure as one in pure ecstasy.

Chapter Twenty

A chiming sound of a text woke Rina up. She lifted her head from Scott's chest as he slept beside her in bed and peered at her phone lighting up in the darkened room. Moving slowly, she slipped out of his one-armed embrace and quietly got out of bed. The hem of the black T-shirt she'd borrowed from him fell to her midthigh, but without Scott's warmth she shivered in the air-conditioned room. Grabbing her phone from the dresser, she tiptoed to the bathroom, shut the door and turned on the light.

For a moment she was blinded as she blinked away sleep to focus on the screen. It was four-thirty in the morning and Philippa was texting her.

GM, sunshine. How was your night with Scott?

Rina paused in answering. How did she know she was with him?

GM. Why are you asking me about him?

Philippa's text bubble popped up with a rolling eyes emoji.

Your car has been in the guesthouse parking lot all night. BTW Zurie noticed too and she's looking for you.

Zurie was hunting her down? Great. Leaning a hip against the white counter, Rina replied.

Did you tell her?

Dots appeared and seconds later so did Philippa's answer along with a laughing emoji.

Seriously? No but for the rest of the day I'm avoiding her like bad shellfish. Love you but I'm not lying to my boss.

Rina answered with a heart emoji and closed out her text messaging app. Avoiding Zurie this morning was probably a good idea for her, too. One, she hadn't had her tea. Two, she needed a moment of silence in the shower. Three—she wanted to hold on to the perfect memory of last night with Scott for a while longer. The best way to accomplish all of that was to leave now before Zurie found her.

After taking care of the essentials and brushing her teeth with one of the complimentary prepasted toothbrushes the guesthouse offered, she slipped out of the bathroom. Using the lit-up screen on her phone for light, she made her way to the bench at the end of the bed and picked up her folded dress.

The sheets rustled. Scott sat up in bed and turned on the bedside lamp. His hair was messy. His eyes were hooded from sleep, and a faint beard shadowed his jawline and framed the mouth that she loved to kiss. "You're up?" His low husky voice settled inside of her raising goose bumps on her skin. Blinking sleepily, he raked his hand through his hair, and muscles tightened in his arm and bare chest. "What time is it?"

"Almost a quarter to five."

His gaze moved from her face to the dress in her hands. "Why are you leaving so early?"

"I have to go."

He reached for the bottled water on the side table. "Have to or want to?"

"I think you know the answer to that."

"All I know is that you stayed with me last night, which I'm happy about, and now you're in a hurry to leave. Why?"

He didn't waste time going straight to the difficult questions. "It's Belgian waffle special day."

"Which is Ben's specialty. He also opens on Sundays. You normally don't go in until eleven." His eyes held hers as he removed the cap from the water and took a long sip.

How could she explain that *want to* didn't fit anywhere into the equation, but *had to*... That was a different story. Rina walked over to his side of the bed. She tried to keep her eyes trained on his face, but she couldn't stop her gaze from lingering on his chest or dropping to the sheet riding low on his hips. Longing pooled inside of her like warm chocolate, wonderful and sweet. The excuse she'd planned to make momentarily escaped from her mind.

He took hold of her hand. "I understand if you're nervous about us spending time together causing people to pay more attention to your personal life." A small smile tipped up his mouth as he kissed the back of her hand. "But personally, I'm happy about being with the prettiest woman in town."

The prettiest woman in town, huh? She almost challenged his claim with a teasing snarky comment, but what did that article say in the same magazine at the dentist's office where she'd found the pie bars? Something about women needing to embrace compliments instead of downplaying them?

She allowed him to tug her down to sitting on the edge of the mattress. "I'm glad you feel that way, and I'm happy to be with you, too. But for some people, it's going to take a little more time for them to adjust to me having a personal life."

"By people you mean Tristan and Zurie."

She already knew where Tristan stood on the matter. He had concerns, but with Zurie, she'd probably view it as an unnecessary distraction getting in the way of everything from Rina winning the Gwen's Garden contract to paying off the loan.

"Yes. They'll have concerns."

Scott drank more water and set the bottle down on the table. "Concerns are okay, and if they need a minute to adjust, I understand. But I think that adjustment needs to take place on their time not ours." He intertwined their fingers. "What about you?"

Time. She and Scott didn't have a lot of it. Why *would* she let any of it go to waste?

As Scott shifted his legs, the sheet slipped lower. Rina tossed her dress back on the bench seat.

Hours later, as Rina stood at the door clothed in the dress and wedge-heeled sandals she'd worn the day before, Scott laid out a path of kisses from her ear down her throat. "Sure you can't stay longer?"

The brush of his lips over her skin renewed her desire. She'd never wanted to play hooky so badly in her life. "I can't." As she rested her hands on his chest, she intended to push away but remained, her heart beating as strongly as Scott's was underneath his dark shirt under her palm. "I have to go."

He stopped his gentle assault to look at her. "I wish I wasn't busy today or tomorrow morning. Otherwise, I'd come see you tonight, but I'll definitely come by tomorrow night to put up the tiles."

"I'll take care of dinner."

"We can work on dessert together." His sexy smile said it all.

"That sounds good, too."

He opened the door and they indulged in one last slow kiss. Her hand lingered in his, a part of her wishing he would pull her back inside instead of letting her leave. If he had, she could have claimed his kisses had wiped away reason. But in reality, responsibility dictated. She had to leave.

Downstairs she got off the elevator following guests with their rolling bags down the hall into the modern wood-floored lobby.

It was morning checkout time.

On the right, sunlight beamed through a window over guests occupying the navy couches in the seating area. The gold frames around paintings on the walls of horses running and grazing in rolling fields gleamed in the natural light.

On the opposite side, more guests stood at the front desk or waited in the short line.

Across the space in the crowd, Rina spotted a familiar face.

Zurie warmly thanked guests for staying at Tillbridge and invited them to come back and visit. In the midst of directing other guests and visitors around the corner toward Pasture Lane Restaurant and the rest of the guesthouse amenities, her gaze landed on Rina.

Smile. Ignore. Deflect. No. Not this time. This

wasn't about business. This also wasn't a walk of shame. She was a grownup and more than allowed to have a personal life. Rina slid her purse strap higher on her shoulder. Zurie was looking for her, she'd find out why. As she started closing the distance, Tristan walked through the glass front door.

He glanced at Zurie then Rina and his brows rose a fraction. He veered right to Zurie and leaned down to say something to her. As Zurie responded, he subtly guided her around the corner.

Rina paused. Had Tristan purposely gotten in the way or had he really needed Zurie? On the drive home, an incoming call rang through the speaker system. *Tristan.*

What did he have to say? She answered. "Hello."

"You can drop the lemon pie you owe me for saving you from Zurie at the office."

"Saving me?" Light traffic flowed past. She slowed down behind the car in front of her. "Last I heard, Zurie just wanted to talk to me."

"A talk, huh? I can only imagine what the topic would have been. From the look on your face, you were gearing up for a fight."

"You're exaggerating. And if Zurie did have something to say to me about a particular topic, I would have politely told her she needed to adjust to the situation."

"You're right. She does. What's happening between you and Scott isn't any of our business." He paused. "I'm sorry for butting in yesterday."

Surprise had her easing her foot off the accelerator. "What made you change your mind?"

"You did." He huffed a chuckle. "I haven't seen you this angry at me since my G.I. Joes borrowed your dollhouse."

"Borrowed? It was an invasion."

"It was a hostage rescue."

A laugh slipped out of her. "Either way, I forgive you. And I'll bring your pie tomorrow." She never could stay upset at him for long. They were back to their easy relationship. If only she could have the same with Zurie.

Chapter Twenty-One

Juggling two boxes with pies, Rina opened the door leading to the back hallway at the stable. She'd already dropped off pies to Pasture Lane. This was her last early morning stop before driving back to the cafe.

As she walked into the office at the end of the hall, Gloria, the stable's admin assistant looked from the wide screen monitor on her desk. "Hi, Rina." The older brown-skinned woman with silver-streaked dark hair peered over the top of her electric-blue–framed glasses. "Let me guess. One of those boxes has a lemon pie for Tristan."

"As always." Rina returned her smile as she went to the corner fridge. "And I brought over an apple pie for you."

"Oh that's so sweet. Thank you." Gloria adjusted the white sweater hanging over her thin shoulders and partially concealing the front of her Tillbridge navy shirt. "The grandkids are coming over for movie night. They can have some for dessert."

"What are you watching?"

"*Frozen*, for the two-hundredth time." Gloria chuckled wryly. "I thought we'd finally weaned them off of that one, but apparently, they sang it at school and learned some dance movements to the 'Let it Go' song. They can't wait to show us, and knowing them, they'll have us singing and dancing right along with them."

Gloria had the ability to intimidate a grownup with a single stern look, but when it came to her grandchildren, she was a total softie.

"Sounds like fun. Is Tristan in the stable?"

"Yes. He's helping one of the trainers from the movie set with a horse, but I'm sure he'd like it if you stopped in and said hello."

"Okay. See you later." Rina walked out of the office. In the long hall leading to the stable, gold and silver framed photos from the early days at Tillbridge, mostly of her parents, Mathew and Cherie, and Uncle Jacob, hung on the walls. They depicted the highlights of their lives from hanging a sign on the front gate at the opening of Tillbridge to competing in rodeos to happy moments with Rina, Zurie and Tristan.

A photo near the end of the array of her father and

mother in a stadium dressed in cowboy hats, West-ern-style shirts and jeans laughing and embracing each other made her pause. They'd been so happy together. Nostalgia tugged at her heart as she smiled, kissed her fingers and press them to the glass. "Love you."

She walked into the modern stable. As she went down the wide rubber-floored aisle separating a line of stalls on the right and left, a few horses peeked over the top part of the navy Dutch-style horizontally split doors. Their whinnies and soft snorts echoed along with the low drone of the ventilation system.

Near the end of the aisle in front of a stall on the right, Tristan was talking to another man around his age, dressed similarly in boots, faded jeans, and a short-sleeved, pullover shirt. Scott was with them. She hadn't expected to see him until dinner.

Tristan noticed her first. "Hey. What are you doing here?"

Scott turned and smiled. For a brief moment she was rooted to the spot as her own smile took over her face. Her heart kicked up and warmth pooled inside of her as she thought about his promise of "dessert."

Denying the urge to wrap her arms around Scott first, she walked over to Tristan. As he gave her a one-armed hug, she poked his chest. "Someone in-sisted I make a special delivery."

He grinned broadly. "You made my day. Rina this is Frank." He pointed to the man with short, spiky

light hair. "He takes care of the horses that are performing in the movie."

"Hello." Frank nodded. Too much time in the sun
had reddened his nose and cheeks.

The deep chestnut-colored horse inside the stall
snorted. As he shook himself from nose to tail, his
coat glistened.

He's beautiful. Rina couldn't stop herself from
gravitating toward the gelding. The horse put his
head through the top door opening, and she rubbed
along his neck.

"Well that's a first," Frank said.

She glanced over her shoulder at him. "What do
you mean?"

"Nash and Scott were supposed to ride Showdown, but he's been shying away from everyone,
including me."

"You have? What's wrong with you, sweetie?"
Showdown moved closer and stuck his head farther
out. She scratched closer to his ear.

Tristan chuckled. "That's a promising sign."

Scott stood just behind her. He was so close she
could feel his warmth. "He's practically eating out
of your hand. You've definitely got the magic touch."

Memories of Scott's caresses heating up her skin
raised goose bumps. She couldn't look at him. If
she did, Tristan and Frank would probably see the
longing for Scott in her eyes. Rina focused more on
Showdown. "Has a vet checked him out?"

"Yes," Frank replied. "I took him to the vet

Tristan recommended last Thursday. She checked him out for colic, viruses, infections, inflammation—even botulism. I just spoke to her this morning. The scan and the blood tests came back negative. She mentioned it could be psychological, but nothing unusual or bad happened to him on the trip up here. The only thing I can think of is that one of the older horses Showdown lived with at my stable passed away, but that was a couple of months ago. He seemed to be over it. He even worked on another movie last month."

Was Showdown still grieving? Sometimes horses were complicated. At least humans could tell someone what was wrong. Horses couldn't. With Noble Wind, she'd always been able to feel him out and he'd seemed to sense her moods, too. Showdown's liquid brown gaze called to her like a plea. "Can I try to ride him?" The words slipped out.

"I don't see why not," Frank replied. "He's better with an English saddle. Are you comfortable with that?"

Four years. That's how long it had been since she'd been on a horse. She could still hold her own. Right?

Scott lightly rested his hand on her back as he stood beside her.

Learning to face adversity meant starting by trying something first. That's what he'd said. And when she'd taken that chance by not knowing what was ahead, she'd been able to fly. Maybe she would again with Showdown. But shouldn't she get back to the cafe?

Rina glanced back at Frank. "I can handle it." She looked to Tristan. "Do you still have my boots?"

A little over twenty minutes later, she was on Showdown in the exercise ring wearing her tall black riding boots and fresh-out-of-the-package tan riding breeches from sample items the stable had received from a vendor.

Showdown fidgeted and shook his head.

Frank waited off to the side near the entrance to the ring just in case there was a problem. Tristan and Scott each leaned a booted foot on the bottom rung of the white ladder fence surrounding the dirt circle. They watched as she maneuvered Showdown where she wanted him, clearly ready to jump in and help if needed.

Showdown had let her put a saddle on him and hadn't attempted to throw her off. They were fine.

Excitement and a hint of anxiousness hummed inside of her, but she reined it in. "You're okay, Showdown." She patted his neck. "We're just going to hang out for a little while."

Using leg cues, she walked him around the ring. *Legs before reins*. That's how her mother had taught her to stay controlled and balanced while riding. She eased him into a trot then a canter. Time and the surroundings faded away as muscle memory kicked in. She was simply there for Showdown, learning how he liked to move as she cued him to change gaits, turn and circle. He willingly responded, easily going through the sequences over and over again.

Applause filtered into her concentration.

A couple grooms had joined them and were cheering her on. Frank nodded in approval. Tristan and Scott both grinned at her.

A happy laugh bubbled out of Rina. If only she could take Showdown to the pasture and give him his lead to gallop through the field. But she really had to get back to Brewed Haven.

Reluctantly, she halted Showdown near Frank at the entrance to the exercise ring and dismounted.

Frank's expression was slightly stoic, but appreciation filled the trainer's eyes. "Thank you. I was worried that he wouldn't let anyone reach him."

"It was my pleasure." Rina stroked Showdown. "I wish I could stay longer and groom him."

"Next time," Frank said. "At least I hope you'll consider coming back. I don't know that he's ready to work yet, but I could tell he enjoyed having you ride him. I haven't seen him that way in a long time."

Their connection—she'd felt it, too. It excited and scared her. She'd let Noble Wind down in the worst way. Just as she was about to say "I don't know," Scott joined them. The pride and caring she saw in his eyes seeped inside of her.

If she could enjoy a temporary relationship with Scott, couldn't she do the same with Showdown?

"What do you think?" Rina asked Showdown as she stroked along his neck. "Should we do it again?"

Chapter Twenty-Two

As Rina climbed the steps to her apartment, the muscles in her legs and butt hollered in protest. Riding a horse after years of not doing it plus running around the cafe for the last nine hours had taken a toll, but the discomfort was worth it. She couldn't wait to ride Showdown again. With some rearranging of her schedule, she could fit in the time.

She still had little over a couple of hours until Scott arrived for the dinner she'd stocked for them in her refrigerator that afternoon. Nothing fancy—roast chicken and rice pilaf already cooked from the cafe and a salad.

Inside in the entryway, she leaned a hand against the wall and took off her tennis shoes. *Will they still fit?* That's what had crossed her mind when Tristan had produced her black riding boots that morning. He'd even kept them polished for her. But they weren't her favorite pair.

On the way to her bedroom, she flipped on the living room lights. Pausing in the adjoining bedroom hallway, her gaze was drawn to the left. The custom-made boots that fit her perfectly were in the spare bedroom closet. A spark of excitement pushed her toward the open door at the end of the hall. The space with a gray convertible sofa, a small black metal desk and a bookshelf served mainly as storage for her clothes and books.

In the corner walk-in closet, she reached up to the shelf above the winter coats. Balancing on her toes, she took one of the cardboard boxes from the shelf and took it to the desk against the wall. As she set the box down, the beige taped stretched across the top seam curled up on one side like a loose thread. She took hold of it and pulled

Scott used the key Rina had given him and opened the door to her apartment. A light pleasant herbal fragrance was in the air…but not the scent of food. Maybe they were ordering out? The two of them having dinner together had stayed on his mind all day along with her riding Showdown.

She'd looked relaxed, happy and confident, and so beautiful she'd taken his breath away. He could have watched her all morning. It had shocked him when Tristan mentioned she hadn't ridden in a long time.

"Rina?" As Scott walked down the side hall, he peeked into the kitchen. Not seeing her there, he went through the living room to the other hallway. The main bedroom to the right was dark, but a light shone from the room on the opposite end of the hall. He went that direction and peeked inside.

Rina sat on the floor in front of the sofa against the wall. A couple of cardboard boxes with the flaps up sat beside her along with a pair of boots. She was surrounded by open albums, scrapbooks and loose photos.

"Rina?"

Seeing her sad, troubled expression, Scott's teasing comment died on the tip of his tongue. He went over to Rina and hunkered down in front of her.

She blinked as if she'd just noticed him. "I…we're having dinner. I didn't realize it was so late."

As she started gathering up photos of her with a horse, he laid his hand on Rina's arm. "Dinner can wait. Are you okay?"

She hesitated. "No. I rode Showdown today and I thought it was good, but…" Rina looked at all that surrounded her.

Moving some of the books aside, Scott maneuvered into a small space beside her on the floor. He pointed to a picture in Rina's hand of her sitting atop of a horse. "But what? The smile on your face in that photo was on your face today. Weren't you happy?"

"Yes." Her expression grew even more sorrowful. "After the accident, I tried to get back on a horse, but I felt lost without Noble Wind. I stopped riding. But when I looked into Showdown's eyes today, I felt a connection."

He took her hand. "Isn't that a good thing?"

"It was wonderful. I came in here to find my favorite boots for the next time and started looking through my old photos. How can I enjoy riding Showdown after what I did to Nobel Wind?"

"Whoa, hold on…"

"No. Wait. Let me explain. Noble Wind and I were a team. He trusted me to protect him and keep him safe, and I didn't." Anguish filled her eyes. "Maybe I don't deserve that type of trust again."

Scott tamped down the instinct to point the finger at her ex. Blame wasn't the issue. He could understand how she felt about trust. It was a huge part of his profession, too. "Showdown has avoided everyone here but you. His instincts are telling him that you're the one he should form a connection with. Why not trust that? Second chances aren't always easy to come by."

"I am glad Showdown trusted me to ride him today, but it's so hard not to remember the past." Rina looked down at the photos in her hand. "I'll always love and miss Noble Wind."

"Getting close to Showdown doesn't mean you have to forget the moments in the photos." He slipped one of the pictures from her hand. "Tell me about Noble Wind."

She nudged his shoulder with hers. "You don't

mean that. I know you're probably tired of being a good listener and hearing me talk. You don't have to. And I'm sure you're hungry."

A good listener? No one had ever called him that in his past relationships—a few times he'd been accused of the opposite. And honestly, it hadn't fazed him because his next gig was on his mind. But with Rina, he honestly did want to hear her stories and what she thought about food and movies and whatever random topic came up. His current job was still a priority, but seeing Rina, being with her, had become just as important to him. And he actually liked it that way.

Scott lifted their intertwined fingers and kissed the back of her hand. "Like I said, dinner can wait. Tell me about the photos."

Hints of gratefulness were in Rina's eyes as she gave him a wobbly smile. "Okay, but remember, you asked for it."

Chapter Twenty-Three

Rina dressed quickly in a peach fitted tee and yoga pants, lured by the scent of bacon wafting into the bedroom. It was the second thing she'd noticed when she'd awakened that morning. The first had been the cool empty space on the mattress beside her. For a brief moment, she'd thought Scott had left. Last night, after she'd given him a photo tour of her life from diapers to her twenties, she'd actually joked about him running away before dawn.

Nope. I'm not going anywhere... I don't have to be on set until tomorrow afternoon...

Then Scott had given her a kiss that had left her breathless and holding on for more.

Later that night in bed, his kisses and caresses, the way he'd moved inside her, slowing down and drawing out pleasure when she'd wanted a faster pace, had awakened desire and need inside of her in ways she'd never felt or expected.

Rina came closer to the smell of food and Scott's humming. He'd never cooked for her before. Usually, he just got takeout from downstairs at Brewed Haven. She crept forward in bare feet from the living room to the entryway on the right and peeked into the galley-style kitchen.

Barefoot and in the jeans and white T-shirt he'd worn the night before, Scott scrambled eggs at the stove in the midst of chaos. What looked to be clean and dirty bowls sat near the sink on the counter behind him next to a cluster of eggshells. A little farther down, shredded cheddar cheese spilled out of the package and next to it a plate was piled high with crispy-looking bacon.

Scott grabbed a plate from the counter and peeked into the oven. "Shit." He reached inside and pulled out a slice of toast with his thumb and finger. Too hot to hold, he dropped it on the oven door. Swearing softly, he shook out his hand.

Rina covered her mouth and stifled a laugh. *Oh my gosh...* Her boyfriend was a disaster in the kitchen. *Wait...my boyfriend?*

Scott saw her. "You're up already." His expression reminded her of a kid who'd gotten caught with his hand in the cookie jar. Snagging tongs from the utensil holder on the counter, he rescued the toast on the door and the three slices in the oven before they burned. "I was going to bring you breakfast in bed."

"That's okay. It's still a…surprise." He'd managed to make scrambled eggs stick to her best ceramic skillet. *How?* And why wasn't he using the toaster oven next to the coffee maker? Her hands itched to take the kitchen utensils away from him.

But his goofy grin was too darn cute and from the egg and grease stains on the front of his shirt, he'd worked really hard.

Ignoring the mess she walked over to him. "Thank you."

Scott wrapped an arm around her waist, slipping his hand just underneath the hem of her shirt, and skimming over her bare skin. He kissed her. "You're welcome."

The silver kettle started to whistle on the back burner.

"Your tea." Scott set the plate down and poured water into a blue mug with the bag of Positive Energy tea already inside of it.

"Sure you don't want my help?"

He handed her the mug. "Relax. I got this."

Standing off to the side, she sipped tea as he divided scrambled eggs, dark crispy bacon and buttered toast between two plates.

As he poured himself a cup of coffee, Scott's phone chimed next to the eggshells.

Rina glanced at the screen. "It's Wendy."

"I'll call her later." As he handed her a plate and a fork, his phone buzzed and a text alert popped up.

Rina glanced between him and the phone. When it came to her family, a call followed by a text couldn't wait. "Shouldn't you check? Maybe it's important."

"Probably not." Scott picked up the phone and opened the text. "It's just a video." Scott clicked on it.

Soft piano music prompted her to peek at the screen.

Various images played in a video featuring a middle-aged couple. The silver-haired man smiling lovingly at the pretty dark-haired woman resembled Scott.

Rina set her mug on the counter and munched a slice of bacon. "Is that your dad and his fiancée?"

"Yes." Just like in the car on the way to Tristan's that day, his expression remained impassive.

In the final frame, as the image faded, words appeared: *Can't wait for you to help us celebrate the best day of our lives. Love Patrick and Theresa.*

As she ripped paper towels off the nearby holder, the date that froze on the screen caught her attention. "That's next Saturday."

Scott set the phone down. "It is."

Strange. He hadn't said anything about the wedding since their conversation in the car on the way to Tristan's house. But he had mentioned not being needed on the film set that weekend. Maybe he just hadn't gotten around to telling her about his plans. "So are you flying out Friday?"

"No, I'm not going." He stalled her question with a raised hand. "And it's fine. My dad and I already talked about it. Let's eat. Our food's getting cold."

She picked up her mug and followed him to the adjoining dining room. "But if they know you're not coming, why did Wendy send you that video?"

Scott released a long exhale as they sat down at the table. "Because she thinks I should be there."

"And you don't?"

"He's done it enough times, I already know what happens. And how it ends."

She caught the sadness that passed over his face before he ate some of his eggs. "Maybe I shouldn't pry, but if the roles were reversed, you wouldn't let me slide out of giving an explanation." Rina set down her fork. "Cynical isn't your style. What's the real reason you're not going?"

Scott washed down the bite he'd taken with coffee. Outside of Wendy, he'd never talked to anyone about his father's multiple marriages. But whenever he'd asked Rina about her family, she'd shared some difficult things from her past. How could he not be just as honest with her now?

He set down his mug. "After my parents divorced, my father was miserable. When he got engaged to Ruby a year later, he was happy and everything was good for about five years." Scott's mind rolled back to living with his dad and Ruby in North Carolina. During his junior and senior years of high school, he'd had a first row seat to watching their marriage slowly disintegrate. "They divorced and the same pattern happened when he married again, and when that relationship didn't work, he tried again. I think it's time for my father to stop believing in forever."

Rina's turned wistful. "But what if this time, he really as found the one? Don't you want to celebrate his happiness?"

"What if he hasn't? After Ruby, I honestly have to try to remember the names of the women he married, his time with them was the equivalent of a blink. But what I'll never forget is how hurt he was when they didn't work out."

Empathy shown in Rina's eyes. "You can't predict what's going to happen in your father's current relationship. And honestly, that's not your place. But in my opinion, Wendy is right. You need to be there." She briefly squeezed his arm. "The one constant in your father's relationship situation has been you and your sister. I'm sure he needs that now and that's why she's reaching out to you. Family is always there for family. That's what my parents used to say."

"And you feel Zurie has been there for you?" Frustration pushed out the words. "Don't answer that. I'm sorry. It's not a fair question."

"But it's a good one." Rina flipped her braids over her shoulder and met his gaze. "Remember how I told you Zurie was against me buying this building?"

"Yes." He scooped a bit of egg on his toast and took a bite.

"My first Fourth of July at Brewed Haven I'd only been open for three weeks. From the moment I opened the doors, we were nonstop with customers. During breakfast service, I left the kitchen and popped into the dining room. My supervisor at the time was acting as hostess. We had a line of people waiting for tables and all of the staff were busy so I started clearing and cleaning tables as fast as I could. I finished a booth and when I turned around, I saw Zurie escorting customers across the dining room. She still believed I'd made a bad investment, but she was still there for me."

Scott polished off his toast. He could see her point, but Zurie hadn't watched Rina's business go up in flames four times. "I hear what you're saying but unless I'm dragged to Florida, I'm not going."

Rina gave him an all too serene smile. "Okay."

Chapter Twenty-Four

Scott fastened his dark cream slacks then grabbed the silk tie from the king-sized bed. As he walked to the full-length mirror hanging on the bathroom door of the hotel suite, he wrapped the tie around the collar of his white dress shirt. Nothing screamed wedding more than a damn pink tie. How had he gotten himself into this?

Water ran in the sink behind the closed door.

A small smile and a huffed chuckle slipped past exasperation. *Rina.*

He'd mentioned that unless he was dragged to Florida, he wasn't showing up at the wedding and soon after, Rina, Wendy and the Universe had entered into a full-force conspiracy against him.

It had started that night when Rina was helping

hang the new blue wall tiles in her bathroom, and Wendy had called for a video chat. He'd answered, and introduced Rina to Wendy thinking it was a great way to stop his sister from launching into what had become her favorite topic—their dad's wedding. The next thing he knew, Rina and Wendy were chatting away about how wonderful the evite video was, and then Rina had disappeared for a good half hour with his phone. When she'd come back to him, she and Wendy were newfound friends who couldn't wait to meet each other. Later that night, Wendy had sent him a text saying how Rina would make a great plusone at the wedding.

A couple of days later, he'd brought dinner for him and Rina to her place, just in time for the wedding movie marathon on television, three of them. One just happened to be about a father hoping his son would make it to his wedding, and Rina had cried happy tears on his shoulder during the predictable ending.

Then came the day when he'd been completely outmaneuvered. During a break in helping Kyle figure out the mechanics for a couple of new stunts being added to the film, a message from Rina had chimed in on his phone. The opening of the video of her and Philippa laughing and drinking cocktails at a clothing store had made him smile. Then whoever had been filming them had pulled back and focused on a full shot of Rina.

The bathroom door opened in front of him and Rina stood in the archway.

Her braids were pulled back fully revealing her flawless complexion. A light touch of makeup accentuated her eyes, brought an appealing glow to her cheeks, and highlighted her full lips. The long pink-and-blue floral halter-style dress fit to the curves of her breasts, dipped against her waist and flowed down her hips to her strappy blue sandals. A slit up the left side revealed even more of her satiny-smooth skin.

Watching her in the video wearing the dress didn't compare to actually seeing her now, and just like then his heart stuttered in his chest. The chance to see her like this had motivated him to buy the plane tickets and make the reservation. Along with the chance to have her to himself, away from the cafe and Tillbridge.

She walked over to him. "The suit fits. Wendy will be so glad. She was nervous about it since you didn't get the chance to meet with the tailor. Do you need help with the tie?"

He actually did know how to tie one, but his brain had stopped communicating instructions as soon as she'd walked over to him. "Sure." Scott took hold of her waist. A kiss to her berry-colored lips was off-limits so he went for the second-best spot. He pressed his lips to the side of her neck. "You look amazing."

"Thank you."

Sweeping kisses downward, he followed the light floral scent emanating from her,.

Rina laughed. "I can't tie your tie if you keep doing that."

"I don't see the problem." He snuck in one last kiss near her shoulder before she nudged him gently away.

"But Wendy will." Rina expertly tied a Windsor knot. "She mentioned what time she wanted you downstairs three times when she was driving us here from the airport last night. It's so sweet that you're walking Theresa down the aisle."

The perfect surprise. That's what Wendy had called not telling their dad or Theresa about his arrival. But when they'd had that talk earlier in the week, she hadn't mentioned escorting Theresa. She'd sprung it on him last-minute.

Scott tugged at the knot that suddenly felt too tight. "Maybe it's not a good idea for me to barge into the wedding like this."

"You're not barging in." Rina batted his hand down and restraightened the tie. "Wendy said that you walking Theresa down the aisle had come up in the planning for the ceremony, but since you weren't going to be there, she decided to walk down the aisle alone. Now that you're here, you're giving them a wonderful wedding gift that they'll always remember."

But would it remain a wonderful memory in the years to come or a highlight to another unhappy ending?

As if reading his mind, Rina cupped his clean-shaven cheeks. "It's a happy day. Stop worrying for your father and just be here for him."

She was right. Now that he was there, he needed to get on board with the celebration. "A kiss from you would help." Tempting fate he leaned in.

Rina swayed back and placed her finger on his lips. "Not until after the ceremony."

As the tall dark-haired usher escorted Rina to the front row of chairs arranged on the wood deck overlooking the crystal blue ocean, she received more than a few curious stares from the two-dozen or so people seated on either side of the aisle in the white foldable chairs. But she hardly noticed, her mind and heart still full from what had happened a few minutes ago.

Scott had been adamant about Theresa, who he had never met in person, seeing him before the wedding started, and honestly, she'd agreed with him.

Wendy had relented, sneaking them both into the small meeting room downstairs where Theresa was taking photos before the ceremony. Stunning in a short white vintage dress with a lace bodice and tulle skirt, the enchanting bride with a pale pink flower in her hair glowed in front of the camera.

As soon as Theresa spotted Scott, her smile turned even more radiant as she hurried over to him. When he'd hugged her, she'd started crying. That had started a leak-fest with Rina, Wendy and the wedding planner for the hotel dabbing at their eyes with tissues trying not to ruin their makeup.

Rina smiled her thanks to the usher and took a seat on the groom's side in the third of the five empty chairs. She wouldn't be alone for long. Wendy would join her soon, and then Scott would, after he performed his role in the ceremony.

A string quartet on the far left of the simple wood arch draped with white fabric and flowers played soothing music that blended with the sound of the waves. With the clear blue sky adding to the backdrop, along with the light ocean breeze, it really was the perfect day for an afternoon beach wedding.

Images of her own wedding years ago rose in her thoughts. She'd tried to convince herself that it didn't matter that her family wasn't there, but as she'd walked down the aisle of the 24-hour wedding chapel in Vegas, her heart had grown heavy with every step.

If she ever got married again, it would happen at Tillbridge. When she was younger, she'd always envisioned a country wedding with lace dresses, cowboy hats, bouquets with wildflower accents, lots of dancing and a horse-drawn wagon with a just hitched sign attached to it.

As Wendy slipped into the seat next to Rina she released a breath. The pink flush in her cheeks almost matched the color of her midthigh sheath dress.

"You okay?" Rina asked.

"Just a little winded." She flipped her blond hair

over her shoulders and fanned her face. "We had a minor bridal emergency. You know the saying— something old, something new, something borrowed, something blue? Theresa left the blue part at her house. I had to go upstairs and get my blue bracelet."

"Didn't you take the elevator?"

"On the way up, yes, but it was taking too long on the way back. I had to run down three flights of stairs."

A balding light-haired man wearing a blue suit and a minister's sash walked out of the side glass door with Scott's father.

Patrick, a silver-haired, leaner version of Scott, looked handsome and distinguished in a tailored dark cream-colored suit with a pink boutonniere, light cream tie, and deep tan dress shoes. He paused on the right side of the arch while the minister stood farther back in the center.

Patrick glanced over at Wendy and smiled broadly. His gaze shifted to Rina a moment, and his expression grew slightly puzzled as if he was trying to place who she was.

The orchestra played the familiar opening to "Here Comes the Bride" and everyone stood.

Rina was torn between which to catch a glimpse of first. Scott with Theresa or the look on his father's face when he realized who was walking Theresa down the aisle. She was drawn to the latter.

Patrick's expression changed from solemn to clearly surprised. He looked to Wendy.

Smiling tearfully, Wendy blew Patrick a kiss.

He tapped the middle of his chest over his heart and sent one back to her. His gaze shifted downward. When he looked back up his eyes were bright as he watched who were probably two of the most important people in his life come toward him. Happiness, amazement and love played across his features.

Theresa glowed with her own happiness. She took a step and wobbled a tiny bit in her white high-heeled pumps. A brief moment of panic crossed her face. As Scott securely held her arm, he leaned down and whispered something that made her laugh.

Making people feel at ease, he was so darn good at that. The sweet moment loosed tears from Rina's eyes.

Wendy nudged her, holding out her pack of tissues.

Rina slipped one out and patted her cheek.

At the decorated arch, Theresa slipped her arm from his. Scott and his father shared a brief but tight backslapping hug.

"Love you, Dad."

Joy and pride hovered in Rina's chest in hearing his low-spoken words to his father. Even though Scott might have had a few doubts about the wedding, he'd come through beautifully.

Scott sat down next to her and leaned in close.

"Thank you," he whispered. Then he kissed her cheek and intertwined their fingers on his thigh.

Soft emotions enveloped her heart as tightly as he held her hand. Next week, next month, they might not be together, but in that perfect moment, Scott was hers and she was his.

Chapter Twenty-Five

At the reception in the hotel ballroom with a larger group of friends and acquaintances, Patrick and Theresa were in their own world, swaying to slow music on the dance floor. He leaned down and said something to her. She responded and he laughed.

Rina danced with Scott a few feet away. She looked up and studied his face. Did he realize that his laugh, his smile, his mannerisms were pretty much identical to his dad's?

Scott smiled at her. "Why are you staring at me like that?"

"I'm imagining you in your late fifties."

"Oh really?" He chuckled. "How do I look?"

"Not bad."

"Good to know. When I see you in your fifties,

you're definitely still hot with just a few streaks of gray in your hair."

"Whoa. Hold on a minute. Hot, I'll take that. Streaks of gray. No. There's no shame in hair color. I'm either dying my hair black or going silver all the way, like your dad."

Scott's gaze shifted to his father, and his grin faded a little with a concerned expression.

She stroked his nape. "You did a good thing by being here. You made your father and Theresa so happy today."

He focused back on her. "I just hope—"

Rina rested her fingers against Scotts lips, cutting him off. "If doubt is a part of whatever you're thinking right now, don't say it. Just wish them well."

Scott took her hand, kissed her palm and laid it to his chest. "You're right. And I do. I also have a second wish."

"What?"

"I wish the party would end so we can go upstairs and be alone in our hotel suite."

The need smoldering in his eyes made her heart skip beats. The two of them alone for the rest of the night—she wished for that, too. "They haven't cut the cake yet so you'll have to hold out a little longer."

Past the round white linen–covered guest tables surrounding the dance floor, a white cake on three staggered stands was the centerpiece of the round table in the corner. As a tribute to the couple meeting at a bed-and-breakfast that harvested its own maple syrup, a vine of maple leaves and pink flowers connected the tiers. The maple syrup theme carried over into the gifts for the guests. Everyone had received a two-ounce jug of maple syrup labeled with the words *The Sweetest of Unions* arced underneath Patrick's and Theresa's names.

Across the room, a couple walking out the open glass door onto the deck caught her eye.

He stroked his hand up and down her back. "How about a walk on the beach?"

"I'd like that."

Outside, on the deck, a breeze from the ocean feathered over her raising goose bumps on her arms. She shivered.

Scott shrugged out of his jacket, and as he held it up for her, the silky lining, warm with his latent body heat, glided over her arms. It enveloped her along with his scent—spicy, masculine and appealing. It was almost as good as being in his arms. After stowing their shoes and his socks on a shelf with square openings that was outside for that purpose, he'd rolled up his pant legs, and they walked down the wood stairs leading from the deck.

He held her hand as she gathered up the hem of her dress that clung and billowed around her legs. Sinking into cool sand that caved and tunneled around her feet, they walked toward the dark blue ocean. With each step the music from the reception faded into the rumble and crash of the waves.

They paused a little farther down and Scott stood

behind her, widening his stance as he embraced her. He leaned in and the heat from his mouth brushed over her cheek along with the cool breeze filled with the sweet salty smell of the ocean. "Warm enough?"

"Yes." As he kissed the side of her neck, she wrapped her arms around his and leaned into his strength.

Moonbeams cast a pale glow over the surface of the water reflecting in the whitecaps and foamy swirls and the waves washing up and receding on the sand.

Her breathing naturally joined with the rise and fall of his chest at her back and contentment settled over her. Tillbridge was magical with its trees, rich green pastures and open sky, but so was the endless view of the ocean. She hadn't been to the beach in ages, and not with anyone like this.

She glanced up at Scott. If she could have bottled the peacefulness she saw and felt from him along with his warmth and strength, she would have.

He looked down and his gaze moved as if he was taking in every feature of her face. "What are you thinking?"

She stroked his cheek and his faint beard grazed over her palm. "I wish we didn't have to leave tomorrow."

Scott lost himself in the honesty reflected in her eyes. He'd been thinking the same thing, wishing for one more day with her away from everyone and everything that demanded they take their attention away from each other.

Great minds think alike...

It didn't sit like some easily thrown out cliché to him anymore. They easily talked about the same things, found humor in the same things and had their own inside jokes. They could communicate with each other through a look or a single word. With Rina he could just relax into what felt natural and real. He'd never had this with anyone else. Had his dad found this with Theresa? Is that what made it so different for his father that he'd risk disappointment in finding love and forever for the fifth time?

Moving in unison, Scott leaned in as she tipped her chin up. She tasted of berries, champagne and her own natural sweetness.

Cocooned in the shadows and her shielded from view by his body, he cupped one of her breasts, tracing over its peak through the fabric. Her nipple pebbled against his fingers, and she sighed softly into the kiss. Need rose inside of Scott. It coursed through him as he stroked his other hand along her waist and down to her hip. He urged her back against his erection that grew even harder as she rested her head on his shoulder and moved her lush curves against him.

His heart pounded in his ears as he brushed kisses down her neck. Her sweet scent, an enticing cocktail that blunted the edges of reason as he inched up the skirt of her dress, bunching the seemingly endless fabric in his hands. Finally he grazed her warm skin.

"Yes." Her moan vibrated into him.

Scott glided his hand to her inner thigh seeking the scrap of blue lace he'd witnessed her gliding up her legs before she shut herself in the bathroom to finish getting dressed. He cupped her and heat soaked into his palm.

Laughter coming closer traveled over the breeze.

Groaning into her neck, he took his hand away from her and slid his other from her breast.

Two couples leisurely strolled along the edge of the surf.

As they slowly passed by, Rina leaned more into him. He fought with his aching arousal as they both took in and released unsteady breaths.

Once the couples had passed, she turned in his arms to face him. Kissing her was out of the question, the desire in her eyes alone made it even harder to bring himself under control. He leaned his forehead to hers.

A short moment later, Rina slipped from his arms. "We should go back inside."

Couldn't they just say to hell with waiting on his father and Theresa to cut the cake and just go upstairs now?

Standing back on the deck, they rinsed off their feet using the lower spigot on the wall and used clean towels on the nearby rack to dry off.

As they walked inside, Wendy hurried over to them with a slightly harried expression. "I've been looking all over for you. Dad and Theresa are ready to cut the cake."

Later that night, Scott unleashed what he'd kept under control for too long. He explored every inch of Rina with kisses and caresses. As he glided inside of her at a pace that was the sweetest of agonies, he lost himself in the play of passion on her face. Gripping her hips, he moved in ways that made her gasp in pleasure, claw into his back and wrap her legs higher around his waist.

As Rina orgasmed, she arched up underneath him. He took her cries into his mouth wanting all of her, needing her more than air to breathe. Her growing climax took him over the edge to a free fall he never wanted to end.

Chapter Twenty-Six

As Wendy halted the black Silverado at the curb in front of the entrance to Orlando-Melbourne International, Rina hurriedly unclipped her belt in the front passenger seat. She and Scott had overslept that morning. To make it to the airport, they'd had to tag team their time in the bathroom then rush to get dressed in jeans, shirts and shoes, while packing their bags.

She glanced at Scott in the back driver's side seat. As he opened the door, he winked at her and grinned. The happy look on his face reflected exactly how she felt. What happened last night and in the wee hours of the morning in their hotel suite that made them late to the airport was totally worth the rush to make their 8:30 a.m. flight.

While Scott grabbed their bags from the back seat, Rina hugged Wendy. "It was great meeting you."

"Same here." Wendy gave her a squeeze. "But a weekend isn't enough. Next time, make it a week."

Rina almost agreed. She'd love to get to know Wendy better. But there wouldn't be a next time. That realization made her squeeze back harder. "Thanks for everything."

"Oh, before I forget. We ordered way too many maple syrups to give away at the reception. I'm sending you some. Maybe you can use them at the cafe?"

"Sure." Hopefully some meant a small box and not a pallet. She really couldn't use a bunch of little maple syrup bottles with *Patrick and Theresa* printed on them, but Rina didn't have the heart to say no.

Scott and Wendy also exchanged a quick hug with a promise to call or text once they landed in Maryland to let Wendy know they'd arrived safely.

Inside the terminal of the small airport, with only their carry-ons and no luggage to check, they made it through security fairly quickly but had to trot-jog to the gate. Out of breath, they handed the gate agent their boarding passes, relieved to have just made the final call for the flight.

On the plane, they found a couple of spaces in up-top storage to squeeze in their bags, and sank into their middle and aisle seats.

As the plane taxied to the runway, Scott turned

his head toward her, leaning in close where she sat between him and a guy wearing a baseball cap who was already asleep. "You good?"

As she looked at him, just like curbside when she'd hugged Wendy, the truth of their situation struck. There wouldn't be another trip like this in their future. Once Scott went back to the set on Monday, his work days would be longer. Between managing the cafe and putting the finishing touches on her line of desserts for the Gwen's Garden tasting, her schedule would be packed, too, making it difficult for them to find time for each other. She also had to find a permanent handyman which would be even harder now. Seeing someone else instead of Scott painting a wall, changing a bulb or fixing a leak would seem foreign and make her miss him more. Every moment they squeezed in from now until he left in a couple of months would mark time toward the day they'd go their separate ways.

Rina snapped a picture in her mind, cataloging the waves in his hair, the green of his eyes, the slight bump on his nose, the light and dark shades of blond in the shadow of hair on his lower cheeks and the angles of his jawline. And his firm lips that delivered the best smiles and kisses in the whole world.

As she took in his face, sadness pricked at her heart, but she forced a smile. "Yes, I'm just a little tired, but in a good way." She closed the short distance and pressed her mouth to his, committing to memory the feel of his lips on hers.

"Me, too." He slid the armrest up from between them.

As the plane reached cruising altitude, she used his shoulder as a pillow and closed her eyes. Contentment spiraled her down into a collage of fleeting thoughts, but one floated above them all. How badly she wished for more weekends, more moments like this with him.

Scott shook his head, turning down the flight attendant's offer of something to drink. He didn't want to wake Rina.

He inhaled the sweet smell of lavender and almond oil wafting from her, as her soft exhales brushed over his throat. He wanted to hold on to every minute with her. Just like he had that morning.

Awakening first, he'd realized they'd overslept, but instead of waking her right away, he'd spooned her against him for a few minutes longer, not caring about flights or where they had to be. The only thing that had mattered to him was the rightness of the moment. And how right it had felt to be with Rina at the wedding as they'd witnessed the beginning of his father's and Theresa's life together. Because of his own stubbornness he would have missed all of it if Rina hadn't convinced him to show up.

Scott rested his cheek on the top of Rina's head. He'd heard what Wendy had said about making it a week next time. She wouldn't have said that unless she liked Rina, and the way Rina had hugged his sister at the airport probably meant she liked Wendy, too. Maybe they could go back to Florida. They wouldn't have to spend the entire time with his family. He could find an Airbnb. One with private access to the beach so she could enjoy being by the ocean. Or instead of Florida, maybe she'd want to spend time with him exploring one of the beaches he liked in California. The meaning of that sank in and Scott held her hand a little tighter.

"Ladies and gentlemen…" The flight attendant's message broke into his thoughts.

Rina lifted her head from his shoulder and slipped her hand from his. She glanced over at him. The soft sleepy look on her face reminded him of her waking up with him that morning.

As she stretched her arms out in front of her in the confined space, she smiled and nudged him. "Sorry, I didn't mean to knock out for the whole flight. Did you miss me?"

"Maybe a little."

Later on, as they sat in the terminal waiting for their connecting flight from Detroit to Baltimore, bad news faded their smiles. Mechanical issues with the plane delayed their flight out, a thunderstorm kept them grounded for hours, and rebooking was a nightmare. When they did finally get the last night flight to Baltimore, they weren't able to sit together. Making it to Bolan at nine thirty that night hadn't been the plan. Had all gone smoothly, they would have arrived earlier that evening, having plenty of time for dinner and relaxing on the couch together.

In the open doorway of Rina's apartment, Scott reluctantly kissed Rina goodbye. As she slipped her arms from around his neck, he held on to her waist. "I could stay here and still make my 5:00 a.m. call time."

"You could, but you'll appreciate being able to sleep in a little longer instead of having to get up earlier and drive back to Tillbridge."

If he left now, he *could* get six hours or more of sleep. That and a hit of caffeine would keep him alert enough for the stunts he had to perform. And after their busy weekend, she needed a good night's sleep, too. "I'll come by as soon as I'm done."

"Okay."

Their last lingering kiss was even harder for him to walk away from. Each passing mile back to Tillbridge heightened how much he missed her, and for the first time in his career, he wasn't looking forward to being on set, but he couldn't wait to make the return drive back to see her.

As he thought of Rina and their relationship, a type of anxiety he'd never experienced in all his years as a stuntman mixed with a sense of determination and deep feelings he wasn't ready to define yet. His heart swelled and beat a little harder.

By the time he reached the guesthouse and climbed into bed, he knew exactly what he needed to do.

Chapter Twenty-Seven

Humming to herself, Rina stuck the order tickets under the corresponding grouping of plates in the service window. The kitchen was short staffed, Ben was deep in the cooking trenches so she was garnishing plates and putting together the food orders for the servers to take out to customers.

Darby appeared in front of her. "A customer knocked over their bowl of tomato soup. We need another one."

"No problem." Reaching back, she turned to the steam table, ladled some soup into a bowl and put it in the window. "There you go. Need anything else?"

"Just a little of whatever you had that's keeping you so calm in the chaos." Darby winked at her and hurried off with the soup.

Staying calm in the chaos was easy knowing what she had to look forward to that night, and as for what she'd had that morning, she wasn't sharing.

Discovering the video message on her phone from Scott had been better than a long hot shower and her Positive Energy tea times twelve.

It had still been dark outside when he'd made the video. He'd been walking somewhere, probably to the set as he'd talked to the camera.

Good morning, beautiful. I hope you got some rest. I really missed waking up with you. Tonight... I want to talk to you about something.

Scott had paused and glanced away for a moment, but when he'd looked back, there was a look on his face, intense but sweet. It was the same type of expression Scott usually gave her right before he was about to deliver a tender kiss.

I know. Keeping you in suspense is kind of cruel. He'd laughed. *But I need to ask you this face-to-face. Miss you. Gotta go. See you soon.*

In the video, he'd pressed his fingers to his lips and sent her a kiss. Sitting on the bed in her sleep shirt watching it, she'd grabbed the kiss and sent one back. Then she'd flopped back on the bed, giggling and kicking her feet in the air like a teen who'd gotten a video from the guy she had a crush on. Is that what Scott was now? Her crush...or maybe more?

As she set up more orders in the window, she mulled over the question and what he might want to talk about until anxiety swirled in the pool of happiness inside of her.

"Meatloaf's up," Ben called out.

As she turned and picked up the Monday special from the prep table behind her, déjà vu swept in. Scott had ordered the same entrée the night he'd come in to apologize for running her over. Or as he put it, almost running her over. A smile curved up her mouth as she garnished the plate with a sprig of parsley. She never could have guessed that smashed pies and a broken sink would turn out to be the best things that happened to her that day.

As she set the entrée on the pass-through counter, Darby walked up beside her.

The concerned expression on her face made Rina pause. Did she need more soup? No. Darby looked way too serious for that. A disgruntled customer maybe? Or god forbid, was there another leak in the bathrooms? That would really be some cosmic weirdness considering she'd just been thinking about Scott. "Darby, what's wrong?"

"Zurie's here to see you."

Was that all? Zurie could be a little intense sometimes. Maybe that's what Darby was reacting to? Rina glanced at her Fitbit. It was close to 2:00 p.m., and the end of the lunch rush. "Tell her I'll be with her in about ten minutes."

"She said she needs to talk to you right away. She's in your office."

Rina spotted Zurie through the window talking on her phone. "Can you watch this a minute?"

"Sure." Darby took her place at the window.

As Rina got closer, she could see Zurie pacing in front of her desk. As she shook her head over whatever the person on the line told her, she unbuttoned the blazer to her blue business suit.

It wasn't like Zurie to stop by at the busiest time of the day for Brewed Haven and Tillbridge.

Rina walked into her office.

"Okay," Zurie said into the phone. "Thank you, Gloria. If you hear anything else, call me. We're on our way now."

We're? Where were they going? Just as she was about to ask that question, Zurie looked at her. The concern mixed with sorrow in her face weakened Rina's knees. She'd been speaking with Gloria. *The stable...* Cold despair struck Rina and she grasped the back of the chair in front of her desk. "Tristan... What happened to him?"

"Nothing's happened to Tristan." As Zurie walked over to Rina empathy was in her eyes. "It's Scott."

Chapter Twenty-Eight

Rina hurried through the glass doors of the hospital into the wide corridor. Her stomach clenched around a ball of fear that had formed the minute Zurie had told her the horrible news.

The details still weren't clear. Some sort of accident happened on set.

At the intersecting hallway, she automatically went right, heading for the visitor elevators.

The layout of the hospital was still clear in her mind from when Uncle Jacob had been a patient there a little over two years ago after his stroke. She'd also gone through one of her surgeries there after her accident.

The sterile smell of disinfectant. The halls and spaces clean and functional to the point of feeling vacant no matter how many people were around. That was familiar, too, along with the small voice screaming inside of her, telling her not to walk inside but escape.

As she stepped off the elevator on the fourth floor, Rina slowed her pace, searching for a familiar face in the waiting room to the right or standing in the hallway or near the nurses' station up ahead. She saw no one. Anxiety started to build.

"Rina?"

Owen's voice came from behind her and she ran to him. "How is he? Is he still unconscious?"

Owen grasped her shoulders and aligned his dark brown gaze with hers. "He's awake and they're taking care of him."

"What happened?"

Owen led her to a secluded corner in the waiting room. As they sat in the black vinyl seats, he ran his hands back over his head. "How much do you know already?"

"Nothing really." Admitting that caused bands of distress to tighten around her throat. "My sister told me there was some sort of accident on set at Tillbridge."

He took her hand. "It didn't happen there. The shooting schedule was changed. Instead of working at Tillbridge doubling for Nash, Scott was doing background work with the second unit. They were in a wooded area outside of Bolan." Owen looked around as if making sure no one else was nearby. "I wasn't there, but from what I've heard, there was an issue with an explosion scene. Scott got caught in the tail end of a blast."

Her hand trembled and Owen tightened his grasp. "When can I see him?"

"I'm not sure. Last I heard, he was undergoing a CT scan. They're supposed to bring him to a room when they're done with him." Owen gave her hand a squeeze. "I need to step out and make a few calls. Will you be okay here alone?"

"I'm fine. My sister is parking the car. She's on her way up." Hopefully with her purse. She'd left it on the floor in front of the passenger seat. It had her phone in it. On the way up, she'd thought about reaching out to Wendy, but she'd held off. "Scott's family—have they been called yet?"

"When he woke up, that's one of the first things he said not to do. He wants to be the one who calls them. The other thing he said was to make sure someone contacted you." Owen patted her hand. "Scott's tough. He'll make it. Stay here. I'll come get you if I hear something." He got up and walked back toward the elevators.

He'd been thinking of her when he woke up after an explosion? As Rina closed her eyes only the explosion part of the situation and him being hurt played through her mind. She opened her eyes, erasing the frightening images.

Across the waiting room, people focused on their phones, some sat solemnly side by side. One woman knitted something with bright pink yarn. A man and woman at the far end were talking quietly and smiling during their conversation.

Happiness and pain, hope and helplessness, first cries and last breaths—hospitals were a tangle of contradictions, and she'd always landed on the side with the hardest outcome. *Please just this once, can it turn out differently and Scott be okay?*

Over an hour later, Owen passed by the waiting room but he didn't stop.

Maybe he was going to the desk to check on when Scott would be in his room. As long moments passed, her legs ached from suppressing the urge to go after him.

Finally he came back. "He's in his room now. I need to go downstairs. An intern from the set is waiting with a bag of Scott's things. Go ahead and I'll catch up."

Rina walked down the main corridor reading the signs pointing down intersecting hallways to the right and left. She found the corresponding placard on the right indicating the hallway where the room number Owen had given her was located.

She found the private room and walked past the threshold.

He lay motionless on the bed. IV poles with bags were stationed on the side. Several monitors beeped.

How bad was he? Rina walked farther in, her heart tripping in a bruising rhythm against her ribcage as despair took hold.

"Can I help you?" An older dark-haired woman sitting in a chair near the bed stared up at her.

Rina glanced back at the man on the bed. "I'm sorry." Backing out of the room on shaky legs, she glanced at the placard on the wall. She'd transposed the numbers.

Fear, relief, uncertainty propelled her back the way she'd come. She wrestled with a whiplash of anxiety that had peaked, dropped to basement level, and was now skyrocketing again. By the time she'd reached the main corridor pent-up sobs were consuming most of the air in her lungs.

"Rina?" Zurie hurried over to her from down the hall. "What happened? Did you see Scott?"

"No. I don't know. It wasn't him." Rina couldn't stop repeating the last three words like a mantra.

Slinging the strap to her black purse and the one to Rina's beige bag over her shoulder, Zurie grabbed hold of Rina and ushered her down the corridor, past the waiting room, and down a side hallway.

As soon as Rina leaned back against the cool wall, a jumble of emotions coursed through her, causing a rush of prickling heat, gasping breaths and a burst of tears.

"It's okay." Zurie rubbed Rina's arms. "I got you. Breathe. You have to breathe. Just like that. It's okay. Now, tell me what happened."

As quickly as they came, the tears started to subside, and Rina swiped them from her cheeks. What happened? She wasn't even sure. "I walked into a patient's room, and there was this really injured man. I thought it was Scott, but it wasn't. Oh Zurie, I could have lost him today just like I did Xavier."

"But you didn't." Zurie glanced at someone in the adjoining hallway. She turned Rina toward the nearby restroom with a single toilet, mirror and sink. Once they were both inside the small space, she locked the door. "Rina, listen to me. If you can't get Xavier or that injured man you just saw out of your mind, we have to leave."

"Leave? But I haven't seen Scott."

Zurie grasped Rina's hands. "Scott is here. He's alive. He's hurting and he needs you, but not falling apart like this."

Zurie was right. Scott was waiting for her and instead of being there for him, she was crying her eyes out. "I'm being ridiculous. I don't know why my emotions are all over the place."

"Because you're human." Zurie dug through her purse, pulled out some tissues, and handed them to her. "And maybe because you really care about him."

Rina dabbed her eyes. "I do."

Compassion came into Zurie's face. "Your imagination has probably been in overdrive since you found out Scott was hurt. When you saw that poor man in the hospital bed and thought it was Scott, your worst fears were confirmed. After you realized it wasn't him, your emotions were pulled an entirely different direction. After going through all of that, you were due for an outburst."

Rina blew her nose into a fresh tissue. "Thanks. I needed to hear that."

"You're welcome." As if on impulse, Zurie gave Rina a one-armed hug.

Rina leaned against her, reminded of the much younger Zurie. The one who'd chased monsters from under her bed when she'd been scared, bandaged her scraped knees after she'd fallen and soothed away her disappointments with compassion.

Zurie ended the hug first. "So what do you want to do now?"

Rina turned and looked at herself in the mirror. She wanted to see Scott, but she had some fixing up to do first. "Got any eye drops?"

Chapter Twenty-Nine

Scott sat up in the hospital bed with his right leg propped on a pillow, feeling as if his head was over-stuffed with cotton. The entire right side of his body, from the bandage on his temple to the angry cuts on his cheek and arm to his bruised ribs and his strained knee pulsed with a pain that was blunted by the pills they'd given him for relief. He swallowed, fighting the lack of moisture in his mouth.

"Can you hand me that?" He pointed with his left hand at the plastic cup of water on the nightstand.

Owen gave it to him. "Need anything else?"

"Where's Rina?" Scott took a long swallow from the cup. "Is she on her way?"

"She's here but..."

"But what?" The pain in Scott's head started to leak past the numbness as he waited for an answer.

"I just saw her down the hall. But she's really shook up."

"Rina's upset and you left her alone?" The instinctual need to get up and find her made Scott sit up, tensing the muscles in his leg. The pain that radiated through his right side kept him in place. He sank back against the pillows. "Did you tell her that I'm okay?"

"Of course I told her. And she's not alone. Her sister is here." Owen's conflicted expression revealed there was more to say.

"Will you please stop going around in circles and just tell me what's going on with her."

Owen's gaze dropped and then he looked at Scott. "I think she's not here with you now because of something that happened to someone else."

"Who?"

"Some guy named Xavier. I heard her telling her sister that she almost lost you like she'd lost him. That's all I'm saying."

Xavier? Why was Rina crying and talking about her ex with her sister?

A quiet knock at the door drew their attention.

For a brief moment, as he navigated through his fogged-up brain, Scott thought he saw Rina walking into his room, but it was Zurie.

"Hi, sorry to interrupt." She smiled politely at

Owen then focused on Scott. "I just wanted to stop by and see how you're doing."

"I'm a little banged up, but the doctors say I'll survive." He couldn't stop himself from glancing behind her at the door. "Is Rina with you?"

"Yes, she's…"

"Right here." Rina came into the room and dropped her beige purse in a chair near the side of the bed.

Owen's gaze skirted over the two women before he looked to Scott. "I'm going to grab some coffee and update Kyle. I'll check on you later."

"I'm going to step out, too." Zurie looked to Scott. "I hope you start feeling better soon." Her gaze shifted to Rina. "I'll be downstairs in the lobby."

"Thanks." Rina gave Zurie a small smile and looked to Scott. "How are you?" Owen had been telling the truth about her crying. Her eyes were slightly puffy and a little red.

"I've had a rough day."

"Were you playing with sharp objects again?"

He reached out to her with his left hand. She took it and came to the bed.

Her fingers were ice cold as he tightened his grasp.

"Yeah, guilty as charged. I'd feel a lot better if you'd let me hold you."

"Is that allowed? I don't want to cause any more damage."

"You won't."

"Are you sure?"

"Positive." It would hurt like hell to hold her, even on his non-injured side, but having her next to him would be worth the pain.

Rina slipped off her tennis shoes. She went to the left side of the bed and sat beside him.

The dipping of the mattress caused twinges, but as she studied his face, he smiled through the discomfort. She leaned in, and he cupped her cheek urging her closer for a kiss. As soon as her lips pressed to his, relief poured through him. She was the only drug he needed. As he deepened the kiss, she laid her hand on his right side along his ribcage and fiery pain spread underneath his hospital gown.

He sucked in a breath.

Rina snatched back her hand. "Oh."

"I'm fine." He laid his forehead to hers for a moment. "I'm just a little tender."

Her bottom lip trembled slightly as her hand hovered above him as if she was unsure where to touch him. "Owen said you were in some type of an explosion. What happened?"

Owen said she was already upset. Would knowing the details make it worse or better for her? But Owen had mentioned one of the outlets that thrived on salacious news had initially reported that he and Nash were dead. All kinds of rumors were probably floating around by now. She needed to hear the truth from him.

Scott sank back more on the pillows and took her

with him. She lay her head on his shoulder. "We were filming at a secondary set today. During rehearsal, it was decided that one of the devices for an explosion sequence needed to be moved a couple of yards over, but it wasn't."

The memory formed in his mind of running past a large tree, anticipating the charge to go off on the left and all of sudden seeing the flash on his right. If he would have hit a tree instead of landing in the underbrush, a mild concussion and bruised ribs wouldn't have been the worst of his injuries.

"I'm so glad you're okay." Rina's voice cracked as she whispered to him. Her hand drifted right on his chest and he flinched. "I'm sorry."

"Relax. It's just a twinge."

"Are you sure being next to you like this is safe?"

Safe. Scott knew what Rina meant, but as her unsteady exhale vibrated into him, it resonated in a different way.

If he hadn't gotten injured, right now, he'd be at Rina's place, asking her to be his girlfriend, and to take the limits off their relationship to see where it led. On the van ride over to the set that morning, he'd envisioned her saying yes. He'd also imagined waking up next to her in his bed in California. Of walking through the doors of Brewed Haven in the future after finishing a job someplace and seeing Rina's face light up when she spotted him and hearing her happy laugh. He'd never had the experience of someone special waiting for him to come home. And he easily saw Rina as the one.

Scott tipped up Rina's chin with his fingers. Concern, relief and caring—he saw it all in her sepia-brown eyes, but the one thing he'd never wanted to see in them was sadness or pain that he'd caused. And he'd done that today. He pressed his lips to her forehead. "Yes. It's safe."

He worked in one of the twenty-five most dangerous professions. This wasn't the first time he'd gotten hurt and it wouldn't be the last. She'd already been through too much with Xavier. Rina deserved to live a quiet peaceful life with someone who'd be there for her 24-7 in Bolan, repairing leaks and fixing broken things in her cafe. Not someone who would break her heart like he would…if he stayed in her life.

His physical and mental pain melded together. Was this the crucial moment where his father had always failed in his past relationships by deluding himself into believing that he could make something work when he couldn't?

Resolve rose from Scott's heartache. He wouldn't make the same mistake with Rina.

Chapter Thirty

Zurie brought her gray two-door Mercedes to a halt in front of Brewed Haven.

At almost nine thirty, the cafe, along with the rest of the businesses on Main Street, was closed for the night.

Rina unbuckled her belt in the front passenger seat. The weariness inside of her made her feel as if she'd been gone for days not hours, but she was too wired for sleep. "Thanks for staying with me at the hospital. I know it took a chunk out of your day."

"It was important." Zurie glanced over at her. "Tristan and I weren't going to let you go through this alone. He would have come to the hospital but the false story about Nash Moreland dying in an accident at Tillbridge caused a big headache."

"What happened?"

"You have enough to worry about." She glanced to the left at Brewed Haven. "And Philippa's waiting for you."

"She is?" From where Rina sat she couldn't see her, but she did recognize her red compact parked along the curb farther up.

Zurie gave her a ghost of a smile that seemed a little sad. "Talking to Philippa is what you need right now. I'll call you later."

"Okay." Rina got out, and as Zurie drove off, she walked to the side of Brewed Haven. Philippa sat at one of their usual talking spots when she came to visit—the landing in front of the door.

A street light illuminated the steps.

As Rina climbed up, Philippa stood and silently waited for her to get to the top. Philippa's casual black sleeveless jumpsuit and matching jeweled flip-flops made Rina long to change out of the Brewed Haven shirt and jeans she'd had on since six that morning.

Her big hug caused Rina to release a long breath as she hugged her back. "How long have you been here?"

"Not long. Zurie called me before you two left the hospital, so I timed it."

A twinge of guilt hit Rina. "I'm sorry. I should have called you."

"That's okay."

She really had meant to reach out to Philippa, but at the hospital, her attention had been fully on Scott.

He'd finally reached out to his family, and he'd convinced them not to fly to Maryland. She'd assured them she'd be there for whatever Scott needed. After dinner with him at the hospital, she'd climbed back in bed with him like he'd insisted and ended up dozing off until visiting hours ended.

Philippa laid a hand on Rina's shoulder. "I'm here for you. What do you need me to do?"

Rina glanced down at the half-full wineglass off to the side on the step. "Can you pour me one of those while I change?"

A quick shower later, Rina sat in the corner of the landing near the door in yoga pants and a loose shirt. She nibbled a saltine from the small plate of crackers, sliced apples and cheddar cheese Philippa had brought her with the promised glass of red wine. She was worried about her drinking on a near-empty stomach after all she'd been through.

Philippa sat on the first step turned partially toward Rina, leaning back against the grill-style metal railing as she sipped wine. Rina had just finished telling her how Scott was injured. "I'm glad he's okay. How long does he have to stay in the hospital?"

"If he doesn't develop any complications, just a couple of days." The relief from that sent a small shiver through Rina causing her hand to slightly tremble as she took a sip of wine.

"How are you holding up?"

From the look on Philippa's face, she already had an idea. "Zurie told you about my outburst, didn't she?"

"She mentioned you had a small one."

"I really should have done a better job of holding it together."

"A better job? Remaining calm isn't exactly the go-to emotion when you find out your boyfriend was in an explosion."

"I kind of freaked out."

"And?"

"I mentioned Xavier."

Philippa's brow crinkled in the silence. "What were you thinking about when you mentioned him?"

During the thirty-minute ride back to her apartment from the hospital, Rina had let herself work through it. "I realized that I could have lost Scott." She took a sip of wine and it melted the remnants of that fear. "I also realized I could have missed another chance to resolve things before the relationship ended like it had with Xavier. My last memory of Xavier is us arguing with each other. Even though I was disappointed in him and I was planning to leave, I didn't see anger in the way we'd end things. I cared about him. I really hope he knew that."

Philippa dabbed away a few tears with her fingers and sniffed. "You've never mentioned that before. I'm sorry that's been haunting you all this time."

Rina sipped more wine. "I never realized it until now." She also hadn't realized just how much it meant to have Scott in her life. Or how deeply she was in love with him.

Philippa topped off her own glass.

"So how do you want to resolve things with Scott?"

Rina walked through the lobby of Tillbridge Guesthouse, carrying a canvas bag with two take-out boxes inside of it.

At six thirty in the morning, a few early risers headed to the gym while staff cleaned and straightened the area.

Were the waffles and bacon still warm enough? Maybe she should swing by Pasture Lane and heat them up again? No. She'd do it after she delivered the good news to Scott.

He'd been discharged from the hospital two days ago. Taking him to her place hadn't been the best option because of the stairs so he'd gone back to his room at Tillbridge. But he'd been so quiet and distant lately. Being in pain probably had a lot to do with it. And being cramped into a one-room space probably wasn't helping his morale, but she'd come up with the perfect solution. Or at least Tristan had.

Late yesterday afternoon, after Scott had encouraged her to go home rather than watching him sleep, she'd gone by the stable to ride Showdown. Afterward, while she'd been brushing him down in the grooming stall, Tristan had stopped to talk to her and the topic of Scott had come up. He'd offered his cottage as a place for Scott to stay since he and

Chloe were spending more time at the house, and she'd gladly accepted.

The guest room bed was larger and there was a sectional for Scott to lounge on in the living room. Having access to a kitchen and a washer and dryer would also make things easier for him while he recovered, and he could have a bit of a social life, too. Owen and other members of the cast and crew could stop by as a group and see him when they weren't working. It was also the perfect relaxed space for she and Scott to talk about their future as a couple. The other night, Philippa had asked how she wanted to resolve things with Scott—the answer was easy now that she realized she was in love with him.

Giddiness made her heart pound just as hard now as it did when she'd admitted it to Philippa. It scared her a little. What if he didn't feel the same way? But when she'd rewatched the video he'd sent her before the accident, his expression, the way he'd said he needed to talk to her face-to-face, maybe he felt the same way about her too?

They'd have to make some compromises and juggle their schedules to keep growing their relationship. They could do it if he was willing to come see her in between jobs and she made time to see him in California. With prior planning, she could also visit him wherever he was. She wouldn't mind putting her passport to work, flying to some exotic locale to be with him.

At the door to Scott's room, Rina took the paper

sleeve with the keycard from the back pocket of her jeans. She knocked before running the card through the reader and opening the door. He wasn't expecting her until later that afternoon and was probably sleeping or just waking up.

But Scott was already up, dressed in jeans and a pullover shirt. A surprised expression crossed his face along with something she couldn't quite place.

His suitcase and a stack of folded shirts sat on the made bed. Did he already know about the cottage? No, Tristan wouldn't have told him before she had. Would he? "You're packing. Are you going somewhere?"

Scott rolled up a shirt and tucked it in the corner of his bag. "Yes. I have to. Kyle's already found a guy to take my place. He's picking him up from the airport when he drops me off there this afternoon."

"You're leaving?"

"I found out the production company was flying me home today late last night. I was going to call you this morning." He limped over to her, slipped the canvas bag from her slack fingers, and guided her farther into the room. After setting the bag down beneath the television, he leaned against the edge of the dresser. "I know it's sudden. But now that I don't have a job, it doesn't make sense for me to be here anymore."

Didn't make sense? Shock and uncertainty kept her silent as he took her hand.

"I enjoyed our time together, but I have to heal

up so I can get back to work. The place for me to do that is home, not here. I know we're ending things sooner than planned, but me being laid up with an injury and you waiting on me—" He offered up a shrug with a nonchalant smile she'd never received from him before. "That'll get old soon for both of us. It's best that I leave now."

She searched his face, but none of the humor, warmth or caring that she'd witnessed in the video he'd sent her before the accident or at his father's wedding or even before they'd gone to Florida was there. The key that Tristan had given her to his cottage grew heavy in her front pocket as her heart sank deeper inside of her, shrinking away from the pain.

Rina forced a smile. "You're right. That all makes complete sense. You should focus on what's important. We both should." Rina slipped her hand from his and turned toward the bed. "Do you need a ride to the airport? Wait no. You said Kyle was taking you."

Scott walked up behind her, and she closed her eyes willing herself not to fall apart. He didn't feel the same way about her as she did about him. Falling in love hard and fast. Once again, she'd let her emotions steer her in the wrong direction.

"I really thought we had more time." He cleared his throat. "But…" He didn't finish during the pause.

"But we don't. I have to get back to the cafe." Rina faced him. As she went to lay her palm to his chest, he grasped her fingers and both of their hands rested there together, but he blocked her from feeling the beat of his heart.

Scott looked down at her and his jawline ticked as if he was holding back from saying something. He slowly shook his head and their hands rose and fell on his chest with a deep breath. "I'll miss you, Rina."

Rina took her hand from Scott for the last time and stepped away from him. "I'll miss you, too."

Chapter Thirty-One

Rina lay in bed in the middle of the night, eyes wide open. Her heart beating in the strangely vacant hollow in her chest that had formed four days ago when Scott left. That's what she got for letting her heart take the lead instead of staying focused on reality—the temporary part of their relationship. Tears started to prick in her eyes. Rina flung back the covers. She had to stop crying over him and move on with her life.

She went to the kitchen and took out the large dish of homemade mac and cheese that Philippa had brought over. Comfort food. That's what she needed. Rina heated it in the microwave above the stove, and when it was hot enough, she set it on the counter nearby and dug in. In between spoonfuls, her gaze wandered to Wendy's promised boxes of maple syrup farther down on the counter stacked against the wall.

Enjoying them herself was out of the question. She'd never be able to eat waffles and bacon again without thinking of Scott. With the wedding stickers stuck to them, she couldn't give them away to customers. If there was a way to take the stickers off without damaging the product label, she didn't have the creative energy to figure it out. She barely had enough to prepare for the Gwen's Garden tasting in a week. Would Philippa be willing to take the bottles?

Rina opened one of the boxes and took out a small jug-shaped bottle with a tag hanging from the top with the name and logo of the company who sold it. Tags weren't on the ones at the reception. She read the back of it.

For recipes visit...

Well, it wasn't like she had anything better to do. She grabbed her iPad from the coffee table in the living room and pulled up the website. A few minutes later, she was searching through her kitchen for ingredients. Soon she was lost in the familiarity of measuring, of feeling the mix of flour, butter, water and salt form in her hands as she shaped pie crusts. One swipe of her finger over the screen of her tablet opened other recipes that she'd collected over the past weeks. A burst of creativity hit, and the empty spaces in her mind and heart that Scott had vacated started to fill with a sense of completion.

Hours later at six in the morning, Rina took in

her creations on the counter. Maple nut tarts with maple syrup, a touch of rum and just a dash of lemon juice to balance out the sweetness of the filling. A very berry pie with four kinds of organic berries. A salted caramel, peanut butter fudge pie just because. Who didn't like chocolate? And she'd finally nailed the pear bars. A fifth offering, apple crumble, was in the oven.

She picked up a pear bar and took a bite. Pecans. They added a light nutty flavor to the crust that complemented the fruit. Would Scott approve? Memories flowed in of him tasting her earlier efforts of the dessert at the cafe that night weeks ago. If she would have just said no to him fixing the sink, she wouldn't have ended up heartbroken. But if she had, she might not have created these desserts. The story of her life—good coming from the challenges.

Her phone rang on the counter. It was Zurie. She answered. "Hello."

"Hi. Do you have a minute to talk?"

"Sure. Go ahead."

"Actually I was hoping we could do it in person. I'm in the neighborhood."

Zurie just in the neighborhood at this time of the morning? "Come on up."

Was this visit part of the tag-team effort, Zurie, Philippa, Tristan and Chloe were doing to check on her since Scott left? So far Tristan and Chloe had stopped by for a late dinner at the cafe and insisted she join them. Philippa had come by with food. Zurie

had done her usual. Yesterday, one of the maintenance guys from the guesthouse had shown up at
the cafe with instructions from Zurie that he wasn't
to return until he'd completed any repairs Rina had
needed done. Taking over. It was just Zurie's way.

Footsteps coming up the stairs echoed from outside.

Rina opened the door.

Zurie, cute and casual in a blue shirt, black run-
ner's leggings and gray tennis shoes, stepped onto
the landing. "Hey." She went to hug Rina but stopped
it midmotion.

Rina followed her gaze down to her purple apron.
It was splattered with flour and caramel. And the
shoulder of her sleep shirt was spattered with what
looked to be berry stains. "Come in."

"You've been busy." Zurie sniffed the air. "It
smells like cinnamon. What are you making?"

Rina closed the door. "I'm finalizing my recipes
for my tasting with Gwen's Garden. You're just in
time to try everything, if you don't mind dessert for
breakfast."

"If they taste half as good as they smell, I'm in."
Zurie followed her into the kitchen and kept walking to put her black portfolio clutch on the table in
the dining room. When she returned she picked up
one of the empty maple syrup jugs on the counter.
"Who are Patrick and Theresa?"

Swallowing against the sudden lump in her throat,
Rina took two apple crumbles out of the oven and

set them on a wire rack on the counter. "Scott's dad and new stepmom."

"Are you okay?" Zurie laid a hand on Rina's shoulder. The sympathetic look on her face threatened to let loose the tears Rina had finally gotten under control after a late night of baking.

"I'm fine." Rina pointed to the desserts she'd just removed from the oven. "I think these taste much better hot." She turned her attention to finding plates in the upper cabinet. "Can you grab a couple of spoons?"

Zurie opened the silverware drawer. "They look great. Why did you make two? Are they different?"

"Yes. The one on the left is the recipe for Gwen's Garden. The other has a little something extra in it."

Zurie laughed. "Let me guess. Alcohol."

"Just a little." Rina spooned up the special caramel apple crumble into the bowls and topped it with fresh whipped cream.

Zurie picked up a bowl and dug in, scooping up a healthy amount of cream along with the dessert. She moaned and ate another spoonful. "What's in this?"

"I mixed quinces with the apples. Quinces are kind of like pears. But I also added a touch of apple pie moonshine. It's pretty great, right?"

"It's fantastic." Zurie's excited expression faded. "You can't give this to Gwen's Garden."

"I'm not giving them the one we're eating. I'm keeping the apple crumble moonshine recipe for me."

"You should be keeping all of this." Zurie gestured to the rest of the desserts. "You need to reconsider this deal with Gwen's Garden. Actually, I want you to just call it off."

Call it off because that's what Zurie wanted? When did Zurie start thinking she had that much of a say in running the cafe? Was it because of the loan? Irritation spiked in Rina. "What *I want* is to pay off what I owe Tillbridge, and for that to happen, I need the Gwen's Garden contract."

"No you don't. The money you want to repay Tillbridge for the loan is what I'm here to talk about. I want to renegotiate our dessert contract with you for Pasture Lane. We should have been paying you more and we will. The change will be retroactive to the beginning of the year. We'll deduct that from what you owe us. And you can erase the rest completely by selling Tillbridge the equivalent in shares in Brewed Haven. I brought the papers with me." Zurie hurried to the living room.

She's expecting me to hand over shares of my business and take a handout even though I told her I didn't want one?

Zurie came back with the clutch portfolio. She slipped out two sets of documents and set them on the counter with a pen. "I had the attorneys draw it up both ways—with the selling of the shares or without. All you have to do is choose which one you want, sign off on it, and it's done."

"No."

"No to which one?"

"Both. You may not have faith in me winning the contract but I will."

"That's not it. It's the opposite. I'm sure you'll win the contract, but it's not the best decision. I just don't want to see you make another mistake."

From the looks of this place you, not Zurie, have been making the right decisions. Acknowledge that, stop second-guessing yourself.

Scott's words to her that day in the booth at the cafe grabbed hold. "For the past five years, I've grown from my decisions and learned from my mistakes, and I'm proud of that."

Zurie shook her head as she slid the papers into the portfolio and closed it with a snap. "I should have realized this wasn't a good time for you to discuss business. We'll talk when you're seeing things more clearly."

Rina's irritation rose. "I am seeing this clearly. Working with Gwen's Garden is strictly my decision, but as usual you're butting in where you shouldn't."

"Butting in?" Zurie's brow rose. "I'm trying to help."

"If you want to help, realize I'm the one who worked their butt off to build Brewed Haven. Not you. And if I want your help, including you sending over a maintenance worker to do repairs in my cafe, I'll ask for it."

Hurt momentarily flashed in Zurie's eyes, but it was quickly replaced with obstinacy. "I need to get back to Tillbridge." Before she left the kitchen, she looked back at Rina. "You're right. Signing the contract with Gwen's Garden is your decision. I just hope you don't look back someday and regret what you gave away."

Chapter Thirty-Two

Rina sat alone at the four-top corner table where she'd held the tasting for Gwen's Garden the day before. She hadn't been able to sleep and rather than keep tossing and turning, she'd gotten dressed and come downstairs hours before dawn and when her staff would arrive.

Rina picked up the pen next to the contract in front of her. She'd received the emailed document shortly after the tasting but after printing the multi-page contract, it had remained unsigned on her desk.

As she flipped through the pages, scenes from the day before of Linda taking those first bites of apple crumble and smiling, of Max's expression changing from skeptical to pure bliss after he tried the peach pear bars, played in her mind. In that moment, she should have been thrilled, but she hadn't been.

Zurie's parting shot a week ago as she'd walked out the door about hoping she didn't regret her decision may have played into it. But why would Zurie throwing shade on her choices bother her so much now?

The same longing to talk to Scott that had plagued her since the tasting reared up. She could call Philippa or maybe Tristan, but it wouldn't be the same. Scott had a way of listening and prompting her to see what she'd missed or maybe needed to consider. But what else did she need to see with Gwen's Garden? It was straightforward. Paying off what she owed Tillbridge and continuing to stand on her own. That's what she wanted, and this contract was the fastest way for her to get there. She picked up the pen.

Voices from the kitchen filtered into the dining area. The 5:30 a.m. breakfast shift staff was coming in the back door. Morning sun was just starting to lighten the dark sky to gray.

A moment later Darby and one of the servers came into the dining area.

Darby spotted Rina in the corner. She exuded natural energy as she strode over. "Good morning. We were all wondering where you were when we didn't see you in the office."

"I thought I'd try the view from in here for a

change." Rina set the pen down and picked up her mug of coffee.

"How is it?"

"The coffee's fine."

Darby glanced around and laughed. "No. The view. Anything need to be changed, spruced up or fixed?"

Just like the contract in front of her, Rina couldn't spot any problem areas. "Not at the moment."

"Let me know if that changes. I'm going to the florist to pick up today's flowers."

"Thanks." Rina glanced over the papers one more time then took hold of her pen. Just as she started to write the first letter of her name, she noticed someone in the periphery of her vision walking toward her.

"Hello, Rina."

"Hi." She glanced up briefly at the slim silver-haired man and did a double take. Shock stalled her response. "Oh my gosh. Dennis! I didn't recognize you."

Gone was the buzz cut he'd worn for years. Not only was his hair swept back and hanging past his ears, but he also had a neatly groomed mustache and a beard covering his slightly pink cheeks. Used to seeing him in work coveralls, he almost seemed dressed up in a red pullover and faded jeans, but he still had on his worn black work boots.

He smiled. "I know you're probably busy with

paperwork or something, but I'd like to talk to you if I could."

"Of course." She set the pen and the contract aside. "Have a seat. When did you get back in town?"

He sat down. "Late last night."

And he'd come straight to Brewed Haven this morning? He probably wanted his old job back. And she needed him. It was funny how things worked sometimes.

She picked up her empty mug. "I could use a refill. Would you like some coffee?"

"Coffee would be nice."

"And what about a slice of blueberry pie? I have some fresh ones in the refrigerator." When he was at the cafe, he'd eat dessert morning, noon or night.

"Thank you, but I'll skip the pie."

Dennis never said no to her blueberry pie. "Okay. I'll be right back."

As she filled her mug and one for him from the coffee urn in the servers' corridor, concern sprouted. He did look thinner than when he left weeks ago. Was he sick?

Darby hurried over to her smiling. "Dennis is here? Is he coming back?"

"He said he wants to talk so we'll see."

"I think that's a good sign. I'll grab him a slice of blueberry pie. Do you want one, too?"

"No on the pie." Rina put the mugs on a small serving tray with two spoons. "Dennis said he didn't want any."

"What?" Darby's brows rose then fell with a worried frown. "You don't think he's sick, do you? He looks awfully thin."

Rina almost voiced her agreement but held back. If she agreed, that would open the door for rumors to start circulating. Once that happened, almost the entire staff would be hovering around trying to find out Dennis's prognosis.

Rina picked up the tray. "He actually looks more fit to me."

Back at the table, she gave him his coffee. A thought popped in. "I forgot your fresh cream."

Dennis blew over the hot liquid in his cup before taking a sip. "Don't need it. This is fine."

Now he really was starting to worry her. Dennis never drank his coffee without lots of cream. "Are you sure? I don't mind getting it."

He waved away the offer. "While I was away, I got used to drinking it black."

"Alright then." Growing curiosity dropped down with her as she sat in the chair across from him. He was full of surprises. She couldn't imagine what was next. "It's good to see you." Rina took two sugar packets from the caddy on the table. "Are you happy to be home?"

"In some ways, yes, but it's actually kind of strange. I've been spending most of my time in a tractor trailer hauling cargo."

Rina paused in stirring sugar into her coffee. "You've been hauling cargo in Alaska? You mean like that television show where truckers are driving over frozen roads and lakes?"

"Yes, kind of." He chuckled. "I just finished training on how to handle a big rig. I'm not driving solo yet, but I'll get there."

The meaning of what he was saying sank in along with disappointment. "So you're not coming back to Bolan?"

"No. I may get a place in Oregon or Washington and work in Alaska part-time. I don't know yet. I came back to make arrangements to sell my house here…and to talk to you."

"To me? Why?"

He rested his forearms on the table and linked his fingers. "I wanted to apologize for leaving so abruptly. I should have given you longer than a one-week notice. I'm sure it put you in a bind."

"I have to be honest, I still don't understand what happened. What caused you to leave?"

"Truthfully?" He met her gaze. "Your blueberry pie."

"My blueberry pie? Was it that bad?"

"No. The opposite. It was that good." He held up a hand in defense. "Not that it wasn't great before that, but yours had always been a little different from my wife Nancy's. But that week before I handed in my notice, you'd managed to make one that tasted exactly like hers all the way down to the crust. It was wonderful." His gaze dropped to the table where he toyed with an empty sugar packet. A small sad smile came over his face.

Rina didn't know if she should apologize for making him sad or take it as a compliment that he'd enjoyed the pie. "And that caused you to leave?"

"In a way." He looked back up but instead of sorrow a light was in his eyes. "That pie, reminded me of something that Nancy used to say—perfection isn't always perfect."

During the long pause, a faraway expression came over his face as his gaze traveled around the cafe. "The years Nancy was running the bakery here and I was her handyman were like perfection to me. Working here and eating pies like she used to make was my way of trying to hold on to her. The pie I ate that day made me see that I was settling for what was familiar and safe. I didn't want to look back someday and have regrets. I had to move on."

As they finished their coffee, Dennis showed her the pictures of Alaska he'd taken on his phone. He looked happy.

Dennis stood. "I should go before the customers start coming in."

Rina rose from the chair. "I'm sure there are people who would love to see you. Are you sure you can't stay a while longer and say hello?"

"No. I've got to meet with the Realtor."

They walked to the front door. This was really it. As much as she hated to lose Dennis for good, she was glad for him. "Oh, your toolbox. It's in my office. Do you want it?"

He waved away the offer. "Let someone else get some use out of my old tools. I already bought new ones."

In her office that afternoon, Rina sat at her desk, her mind filled with what Dennis had said and looking back over her own life.

Xavier… Noble Wind… Scott. As hard as it was to lose them, she couldn't have imagined her life without them or the lessons they'd taught her. The importance of not losing herself in someone else's definition of life. To not take what brought her joy for granted and hold it close. To believe in herself and what she wanted and to love.

The line of desserts she'd created would allow her to pay Tillbridge back for the loan that was paid on her behalf and not feel indebted to her family financially. To get her life of independence back. Brewed Haven, the place that brought her so much joy would be secure. And creating the line of desserts had taught her to believe in herself even more. Loving Scott and being with him, that hadn't turned out the way she'd wanted. As much as it hurt, she'd have to learn to accept that, and do what Dennis suggested. Move on.

Rina slid the contract in front of her and picked up the pen.

Chapter Thirty-Three

Rina bypassed the front desk and veered down the hallway to Zurie's office. The door was locked, but she heard papers shuffling and the tapping on a computer keyboard inside.

She knocked but only silenced answered. "Zurie it's me. Can we talk?"

A long moment went by and Rina's heart sank. They hadn't spoken since Zurie had showed up with the two agreements and she'd blown up at her, but she really needed to talk to her. Sitting at her desk with the contract in front of her, she'd realized Dennis had almost said the same thing Zurie had about regrets. She'd assumed Zurie had said it in judgment, but Zurie had looked genuinely hurt when she'd snapped at her. Butt in, take control and give opinions, yes

Zurie did all of those things, but she wasn't cruel. She had a heart. She'd shown that to her when she'd stayed by her side at the hospital with Scott.

Zurie had also never been so adamant about her not doing something like she had with the Gwen's Garden contract. Rina looked up at the security camera near the door. She needed to know why.

The lock on the door disengaged and Rina walked inside.

Zurie sat behind the oak desk staring at her with a neutral expression. "Have a seat."

Rina took a seat in the chair in front of the desk. "I'd like to talk about what happened last week when you came to my apartment."

"What is there to talk about? You made things clear. You want me to butt out. I'm out. End of discussion."

"I'm not here to rehash an argument. Please, just listen to me."

Becoming a wall of silence, Zurie crossed her arms over her chest and leaned back in the chair.

Rina took a deep breath. On the drive over, she'd tried to think of the right words to say. "First, I'm sorry for yelling at you, but put yourself in my position. How would you have reacted if I'd drawn up legal documents for your business without consulting you first?"

Zurie's shuttered expression opened up a little. "I wouldn't have liked it, but now you make the switch. What would you do if you saw me making what you thought was a bad decision? Would you just sit back and let it happen?"

"Honestly, I don't know. From your point of view, you never make bad choices. Only I do."

A stunned look came over Zurie's face. "Is that what you think?" She stood, turned away from Rina and looked out the window at the pasture. "I didn't mean to make you feel that way. All I've ever wanted to do was keep you from harm."

"I'm not a child."

"I know that, but I've been watching over you since you were a baby. I helped you learn how to walk. I taught you how to make your bed and tie your shoes. I helped you with your homework."

All of that was true. Zurie had looked after her, right along with their parents. "I know you've always been there for me. I'm not disputing that."

"Always?" Zurie huffed a laugh. "No, not always. The one time I should have paid attention I didn't, and…"

Rina waited but she didn't finish. "And what? Uncle Jacob bailed me out with money from Tillbridge when he shouldn't have?"

"No. I couldn't care less about that." Zurie's voice cracked. "I'm talking about when we almost lost you."

"You mean the accident?"

"Yes."

Rina rose from the chair. "But there's nothing you could have done about that."

"Yes, there was. I knew you were hurting after Mom died and not making the national team. I should have been there to help you get through it. If I had, maybe you wouldn't have run off. The one time you really needed me, I failed you."

"No you didn't." Rina went over to Zurie, surprised to see her blinking back tears. Not sure if Zurie would accept a hug, she wrapped an arm around her shoulders and gave her a fierce squeeze. "You didn't fail. You kept this family and Tillbridge going when it felt like the world was burning down around us. You helped make sure I had a place to come back to."

Zurie glanced over at her. "If I was doing such a great job. Why did you leave in the first place?"

"In hindsight, everything moved fast with Xavier. I didn't have time to dwell on all I'd lost. I thought he made me feel more alive, even safe, but honestly being with him just gave me an excuse to feel numb."

"I just wish I could have saved you from having to go through all the bad that happened to you." Zurie slipped away to grab a tissue. She sniffed and dabbed the corner of her eyes. "That's all I was trying to do when I came up with the solutions for you to pay the money back to Tillbridge. I'm sorry. I guess I should have respected what you wanted."

The solutions to pay the money back—Zurie's worst ideas ever. *But it came from a good place.* No. That didn't make it right. Zurie had overstepped but only because she'd let her do it all these years.

It *was* time for Zurie to start respecting her choices about Brewed Haven and her life.

Rina grasped Zurie by the shoulders and turned her so they were facing each other. "Yes, you should have, and I forgive you. I don't need you to save or protect me. I need a friend, a confidante, a sounding board, a built-in cheerleader."

"Don't you already have those things in Philippa?"

Rina almost missed the uncertainty that flashed in Zurie's eyes. The night of Scott's accident when Zurie had dropped her off at the apartment, Zurie had said that Philippa was who she needed. Had Zurie thought she didn't want her around?

Taking advantage of Zurie's emotional guards being down, Rina hugged her. "Philippa is my best friend, but she can't replace you. You're my sister. You're the only person I can share my albums and scrapbooks with who understands what every single moment and photo means."

"Okay." Zurie squirmed and awkwardly patted Rina on the back. "I understand. But just so you know, we never have to do the look-over-every-photo-and-scrapbook thing."

Smiling, Rina let her go. "That's what everyone says until I pour up a few cocktails to go with the memories." They were headed to a better place now as sisters, but one final thing still piqued Rina's curiosity. "Why were you so adamant about me not signing with Gwen's Garden?"

More composed, Zurie leaned against the edge of her desk. "Are you sure you want to know?"

"I do."

"It goes back to you and Xavier. What bothered me the most about you being in that relationship is that you seemed to see yourself as less important than him. You were willing to give up so much for so little in return. In my opinion, you're doing it again with Gwen's Garden." She reached out and grasped Rina's hand. "Those desserts you created for their line, I didn't even have to taste all them to know that they're your best work. You should be capitalizing on them, not anyone else."

"I actually have been thinking about how I can do that for myself."

"You have? What are you thinking?"

"It's not a fully formed idea yet. I'm still trying to put the pieces together."

"Would it help to talk about it? That is, if you want to tell me. I promise to do more listening than opinionating." An earnest interest brightened Zurie's face.

It might actually be a nice change to brainstorm with someone. And Zurie was great at developing projects. "If you have time, sure."

"I'm free now."

Rina followed Zurie to the couch and sat next to her. They'd never done anything like this before. "Where should I start?"

"Do you mind if I ask one unrelated question first?"

"Go ahead."

"Why did you and Scott break up?"

That was a question Rina hadn't expected. She pulled up a smile. "Why are you asking?"

Zurie held up her hand. "You're right. I'm sorry. That's not what we sat down to talk about."

"I didn't say that."

"You don't have to. Whenever you don't want to talk about something with me, you smile and change the subject or try to point my attention elsewhere."

"Wait. All this time, you knew that's what I was doing?"

Zurie laughed. "Of course I did. It was so obvious."

Rina turned more toward Zurie. If they were truly going to make a fresh start, she couldn't use the smile, ignore, deflect game anymore to avoid conversations. "Actually, Scott broke up with me. He needed to focus on healing up after his injuries so he could get back to work. He felt that he could do that better at home."

"Really? That's what he told you?" Zurie's brow furrowed with a skeptical look. "I don't know if that's entirely true. Or maybe I'm overthinking it."

Apparently as sisters they shared that habit, but maybe in this case, Zurie wasn't. "What do mean? Tell me."

"Well, at the hospital when you needed a minute

before you went to see Scott? His friend walked by where we were in the hallway."

Needed a minute? That was a polite way of describing her meltdown-ugly cry. "You mean, Owen?"

Zurie shrugged. "If he was the one who was in Scott's room that day, yes. Anyway, when I went to Scott's room ahead of you, I'm pretty sure I overheard Owen mention Xavier's name before I walked in. They stopped talking when they saw me, but Scott looked concerned about whatever Owen had said to him."

"But Scott knew about Xavier and the accident. He wouldn't have gotten upset over hearing we were talking about him."

"No, but he might have been concerned if Owen told him you were upset and had overheard you say you'd almost lost him like Xavier. You were really emotional. Some guys don't know how to interpret that correctly."

But Scott had always been understanding, and he'd never encouraged her to hold back. But she'd also never had a meltdown in front of him. Had hearing she had turned him off and that's why he'd decided to end it? If she hadn't gone in the wrong room in the first place, and gone straight to him, would they still be together now? Sadness plummeted inside of Rina.

Later on at home, Zurie's theory stayed on Rina's mind taking her attention from the rom-com she'd turned on as a distraction. Scott had willingly given up his place in his family's company so he wouldn't be in Wendy's way. Had he made a similar sacrifice, leaving because he believed he was doing what was best for her? The Scott she knew, if he believed he was hurting her, would have done anything not to cause her pain.

A seed of hope sprouted and she picked up her phone lying on the couch next to the remote. Or was she making assumptions based on the Scott she thought she knew. She'd completely fallen for him, but the only thing Scott had ever said to her was that he wanted a temporary relationship. He'd also mentioned before his dad's wedding that his father needed to stop believing in forever when it came to love. She'd just thought he was concerned about his father not finding happiness the fifth time around, but maybe Scott had said that because that's exactly how he felt… Maybe Scott didn't believe in love and forever.

Chapter Thirty-Four

"*Don't go,*" Rina said to Scott as she cupped his cheek.

The of dream of lying in the grass near bales of hay with Rina in his arms was the best one he'd had since he'd left her and flown home to California.

But before he could kiss her, the ringing doorbell yanked him from sleep.

Scott opened his eyes. He lay on the brown couch in his living room with a blanket bunched under him, and instead of Rina, he held a navy throw pillow. A sense of emptiness, almost as agonizing as pain from his injuries grew in his chest…along with his frustration.

Who was bothering him? What time was it? He tossed the pillow, and it knocked over the bottle of pain reliever on the coffee table and an empty pizza box to the floor. As he sat up, his phone that was stuck between the couch cushions poked his hip. He dug it out and checked the time. It was 12:30 p.m. After a restless night, he'd just managed to fall asleep a little over three hours ago.

As he moved to get up, his bruised ribs and hurt knee protested with stabs of agony. Expletives exploded in his mind.

The doorbell chimed again.

He slowly got up. Ignoring the crutches on the floor, he hobbled across the living room. Someone was about to have a really bad day for waking him up.

He opened the front door ready to unleash hell.

"Hi," Wendy stood in the doorway, hair in a ponytail, and dressed in tennis shoes, gray leggings and a light gray sweatshirt top with a pink heart on it.

Her cheery smile pulled a growl of discontent out of him that came out throaty and parched from just waking up. "What are you doing here?"

"That's a dumb question." She stopped to kiss him on the cheek before breezing past wheeling a small suitcase behind her. "We came to take care of you."

"We who?"

"Take a look."

He peeked outside.

His dad and Theresa, twin-like in tennis shoes, jeans and cream-and-blue button-down shirts wheeled suitcases from a black sedan in the driveway down the stone path to the door.

Weren't they supposed to still be on their extended honeymoon?

Scott glanced back at Wendy. "Whose idea was this? Yours or theirs?"

She raised her brows and shrugged. "At this point, does it really matter?"

Before Scott could reply, his father and Theresa were at the threshold. As Theresa walked in, she smiled and patted his arm.

His dad paused in front of him. "How are you?"

"I've been better."

His dad gripped his shoulder. "Well, you don't have to worry about anything now. Your family's here."

Family? Scott shut the door. They got together on holidays. They didn't just show up for random visits. Right now, he wanted to be left alone. Scott turned around, planning to say just that, but behind the smiles, he saw true concern in their eyes.

His father and Theresa had interrupted their honeymoon to come see him, and Wendy probably had a ton of things to do at her job. He couldn't hurt their feelings because he felt like he'd been run over, one-two punched, and kicked all at once.

Suddenly, a mix of gratitude and relief came over him. He swallowed hard and cleared his throat. "Um…if I would have known you were coming, I would have cleaned up and bought some food."

"Don't you worry about it. That's why we're here," his father said, taking Theresa's bag. "I'll put our luggage in the guest room and then we can get started on a list of things we need."

"I guess I'm bunking here," Wendy chimed in. She glanced at the rumpled blanket on the couch and the stuff scattered on the coffee table and floor. "Yay me."

"I can stay here." Scott hobbled toward the couch. "You can sleep in my room."

"No." Wendy and Theresa said at the same time. They ushered him to his bedroom.

He agreed to stay there, in bed, under mild protest. He'd lie there and watch TV for an hour or two then get up. But he fell asleep. At some point, Theresa came in, turned off the television and brought him a glass of juice and one of his prescribed pain pills. Too tired to protest, he took it and conked right out again.

Later on, loud conversation, the sounds of opening and closing cabinets, and a '90s Garth Brooks song came from the kitchen.

Scott limped groggily down the hallway to see what the ruckus was all about. He paused and leaned against the wall, taking advantage of a moment to watch before they spotted him.

His dad had apparently commandeered the kitchen to make lasagna. While he laid noodles in a pan, Theresa washed lettuce in the sink. Wendy stood on the living room side of the counter, drinking a glass of wine, egging their father on as he sang off-key.

When the love song ended, his dad fed Theresa some of the sauce for the lasagna with a spoon. As she smiled her approval, his father kissed her.

The memory of kissing Rina in the barn flooded into Scott's mind. For a moment his heart swelled like it had then from the rightness of her in his arms and the feel of her soft lips under his. The recollection shifted to a new daydream of Rina sitting next to Wendy, fitting right in as he prepped dinner with his father and Theresa. Sadness and longing stirred inside of him.

"Hey! Look who's finally awake," his father called out.

Scott swept away the image in his mind and went to join Wendy. "How long was I asleep?"

"About seven hours," Wendy replied. "You needed it."

He did feel more refreshed than after the nights he'd spent sleeping on the couch.

She pulled the stool out beside her a little farther from the counter for him. "Now maybe you're awake enough to trim that scruff off of your face. You look like an angry troll."

"No I don't." He swiped her glass and took a sip.

Wendy grinned. "Do too." Forgetting about his injuries, she smacked him near his side and he winced. "Oops, sorry."

"Wendy, stop picking on your brother," their father mocked an admonishing frown as he stared at her. "And you—" he pointed to Scott "—put down that glass. No alcohol with pain meds."

"Yes, sir," Scott and Wendy answered, both feigning obedience before they looked at each other and laughed. It was like old times when they were kids getting each other into trouble and keeping each other out of it.

Over the next few days his dad, Theresa and Wendy doted on him, doing his laundry, cooking meals, cutting the lawn. As usual Wendy harassed him and beat everyone at poker, video games and Monopoly. And he enjoyed having them there. Being a family.

The day his father, Theresa and Wendy were flying home, Scott sat with his father on the back deck that morning. He drank a glass of mango and pineapple juice—he wasn't drinking caffeine because of the headaches he'd been getting since the accident—while his father enjoyed a cup of coffee.

Scott sipped from his glass. They'd been there only seven days, but the time they'd spent with each other had felt like months of fresh air he'd needed to breathe and feel somewhat renewed again. He'd miss them.

His father looked over at him. "So what's next for you?"

"Not much until the knee heals up. After that, I haven't committed to anything yet. Kyle, one of the stunt coordinators I worked with, wants to talk to me about an opportunity."

"Sounds like you're going to have a lot of time on your hands." His father drank from his mug. "Are you going to see Rina again? Theresa and I really liked her."

This was the first time he'd had to answer the question. "No. I'm not seeing her anymore. We broke up." He drank from his glass, washing down the confession. Suddenly, the juice tasted less sweet.

"Mind if I ask why?"

"Only if you tell me why you're so curious."

His father shrugged. "You looked happy with her."

"I was, but…" He released a long exhale, searching for an explanation. "Me getting hurt, I could see that it brought up some bad memories for her. So rather than putting her through that, I ended it."

"Rina told you what happened was affecting her that way?"

"She didn't have to. I know how Rina's past affected her. She told me."

His father gave him a puzzled look. "Let me get this straight. She told you about her past, and you assumed she was too weak to handle what happened to you now so you made the decision that the two of you should break up."

No. Wait. His father had it all wrong. "I didn't say she was weak. Rina's one of the strongest, smartest women I ever met."

"Then why did you treat her like she wasn't?"

Scott opened his mouth to object and shut it. That's exactly what he'd done.

His father released a low chuckle. "Don't beat yourself up too much. You're not the first man to make that mistake. As someone who's done it more than a few times, four to be exact, can I give you some advice?"

Relationship guidance from his father—that was a thing Scott hadn't envisioned in his future. He'd also never imagined that someone like Rina would enter his life or that she would have the ability to stop him in his tracks with just a smile.

He'd always valued his solitude and lack of attachment to anyone, but now he just felt lonely. Especially without her. If anything his father said might help him understand what to do, he'd listen.

Scott set his glass on a metal side table. "Go ahead."

"First, remember the lesson you just learned— never assume you know what a woman is thinking or what she wants. Two, realize that you making that assumption points to something that you need to work on in yourself." His father looked him in the eye. "And three, if you really care about Rina, confront whatever went wrong between you head on and fix it. And don't wait until it's too late to apologize to her."

Scott saw his father's conviction. This time with Theresa, his father wasn't searching for something.

He'd found it. "So you learned all of that this time around?"

"With a lot of help from Theresa." His father winked. "And the months of premarital counseling we went through."

His dad really was serious about this marriage. "I can't lie, Dad. When Wendy said you'd finally found 'the one' I was skeptical. But she was right."

"No. Theresa's not the one."

"She's not? You just said she was, not in those words but that's what you meant, isn't it?"

His father shook his head. "Saying you found 'the one' means you're expecting them to be perfect and that's a lot of pressure to put on someone you love. 'The one' in a relationship is you, being all in, and doing what it takes to work things out."

That evening after his family left, Scott drank ice water and watched the sunset on the deck. Even though the chair beside him was now empty, what his dad had said to him that morning remained. Why had he made assumptions about what Rina could handle? The truth sitting inside of him was as clear as the water in his glass. *I love her.* Those three words scared him more than any stunt he'd ever faced. He'd expected Rina to be perfect, and when she'd fallen short in his eyes when he'd gotten hurt, he'd made her the problem and used those assumptions as an excuse to walk away. Yeah, he'd really messed up.

Scott rested his head back on the chair. He'd never had to navigate this before because he'd been in only short-term relationships. There was no "all in" like his father had mentioned in that type of situation. And there also wasn't the possibility of loss because nothing had to be invested. Going "all in" with Rina, if she gave him that chance, would mean he'd have to face the possibility he could lose her in any number of ways just as easily as she could lose him… and there might not be anything that he could do to stop it. But what he could do was put in the work, face the harder choices and make every moment they shared together mean something.

Scott took a sip from his glass and allowed it all to sink in with the ice water settling inside of him. The flip side of that—not having Rina in his life—felt just as cold. He wanted her warmth, her touch as the first thing he woke up to every morning and her face as the last thing he saw when he closed his eyes at night. He wanted to paint walls, lay tiles and fix leaky faucets with her in a place they called their own. And someday, maybe kids, tiny replicas of him and her, who they'd watch grow into their own independence. He wanted "all in" with Rina, and what came with it, more than he wanted his next breath. But by leaving had he lost her completely?

Chapter Thirty-Five

Two weeks later

Rina dug the garden trowel into the dirt. When the
hole was deep and wide enough, she removed the
pink hydrangea, roots and all, from the black plastic pot and set it in the space she'd made for it. More
hydrangeas, dwarf spruces and boxwoods were in
the plant bed in front of the tan-and-salmon brick
trim on the bottom of the two-story white clapboard
house. Once the plant was firmly settled into the
ground, she stood, stripped off her gardening gloves
and walked to the front lawn to check her work.

A mirror arrangement of plants sat on the other
side of the stairs leading up to the porch.

Blue sky and clouds reflected in the windows on

the bottom level of the house and the two windows on the top level below the pitched-roof attic space. A light breeze filled with the scents of rich earth, green and sunshine washed over her, and she breathed it in. This was the first of many wonderful mornings to come in her new home.

After gathering up her garden tools and gloves in the blue bucket, Rina carried them down the side lawn to the small shed toward the back. Dennis had said the space with wood storage cabinets and a tiled floor had been one of his wife's favorite places. As Rina stood at the utility sink nestled into the beige L-counter, gazing out the window overlooking the back lawn, she could feel the love and contentment Dennis and Nancy had experienced there, just like she could in the house. It was soaked into every brick, beam and stud. It gave her hope. What was that saying she'd read in a book a long time ago? As long as the rootstock remains, good will continue to flourish? She was counting on it.

Rina walked through the side door of the house and into a hallway leading to the kitchen. The contractors were arriving that afternoon giving her a few hours of peace. She laid her phone on the beige marble counter over the wood cabinets that had been recently installed. The appliances she'd picked out would arrive tomorrow. Hands tucked into the back pockets of her jeans, she strolled through an archway into the living room where the old drywall was being taken down and new Sheetrock was being installed.

Time rolled back to her and Scott working in her bathroom, laughing as they put up the drywall and tiles. So many times since she'd purchased the house, she'd thought of him, wondering what his opinion would be on something involving the remodel. What would he think of her modern spa-like bathroom? How badly would he have teased her about it taking four tries to get the right shade of sunny yellow for her bedroom—not too bright, but with a softness that absorbed the natural light? If he were still in her life, would they have lingered in bed in the mornings with his needed coffee and her required moment of silence watching the sunrise?

A longing for him rose and she took in a breath, filling the raw hollow space in her chest. Where was he? In Hollywood or some other place on the globe, jumping from a tall building or flying out of one? Reluctantly, Rina let the image of Scott disappear and focused on the house. She would make this space hers, and little by little, fill it with the good memories to come.

Her phone rang and she retrieved it from the kitchen. *Zurie.* They checked in with each other at least twice a week now, in person or on the phone. It was still a work in progress, but the unspoken ground rules seemed to be working. No prying or judgmental conversations, just a brief chat about what was going on in their day-to-day.

Rina answered on the third ring. "Hi."

"Hey, are you busy this morning? Tristan and I

were talking about what to do with the new barn once filming the movie is over. We could use a third opinion."

Including her in decisions about Tillbridge was also entering more in their conversations. Rina rested a hip against the counter. "I thought he wanted to turn it into stalls for Tillbridge or family-owned horses?"

"Maybe. But we'd still like to explore more ideas. Can you come by in about an hour so we can talk about it?"

"Sure, but it might be a little more than an hour. I was digging around outside. I have to get cleaned up."

"Okay. We'll meet you at the barn when you get here."

Rina double-checked the calendar on her phone for what time the movers were coming by her apartment. They were picking up the packed boxes of pictures and memorabilia she'd stored in the guest room later that morning. She, Zurie and Tristan had decided to install glass cases in the hallway outside the Pasture Lane Restaurant. Now the Tillbridge family history of horses and their decades-long legacy of competition as cowboys and cowgirls would be shared.

Close to an hour later, dressed in a fresh T-shirt and jeans, Rina pulled into the half-full parking lot in back of the stable. The film crew and cast, along with the bulk of set security had moved to the other side of the property where the new indoor arena was located.

In front of her, the paddock adjoining the stable was empty, but three horses looked out from the back of their closed stalls. Farther down, a groomsman and a trainer spoke to a dozen or so people settled at the picnic tables in the seating area. Most likely they were guests being briefed for a trail ride.

Rina walked toward the pasture on the other side of the parking lot. As she trekked across the mown grass, the memory of Scott flying out of the barn and running into her started to play through her mind. His face. His easy smile. The way he'd held on to her and the sheet pan of desserts. She stopped the flow of images and the sense of bittersweetness wrapping around her heart. *You're embracing the future, not the past. Remember?*

As she approached the barn, a soft whinny caught her attention. Was it coming from inside the barn? Just as she was about to peek inside, she saw the white-paneled temporary horse stall. Showdown looked out over the center railing.

"Hey, handsome." Showdown snorted a greeting as she gave him a rub. "I would have brought an apple if I would have known you were here. Why aren't you in the stable or with the other set horses?"

"Because I bought him."

She looked over her shoulder and her heart tripped. *Scott.* He was a little leaner since the last time she'd seen him, but his chest and shoulders were still impressive in a cream-colored shirt with pushed-up sleeves. Faded jeans hugged his muscular thighs. When he'd left weeks ago, medication had dulled his green eyes, but now they were clear in the sunlight, and trained on her.

Reasons for his presence, from working on the film again to the one she tamped down as impossible, battled for precedence in her mind. But why buy a horse that was finicky about who rode him? "You bought Showdown." She faced him. "Why?"

"Because he's tired of traveling around and coming back to an empty place. It took him a while to realize it, but he's ready to call one spot home with the one that means more to him than anyone else." Scott stopped in front of her. "But he messed up in a big way. And whether or not he gets what he wants depends on one thing."

Scott was talking about himself, but Rina controlled the hope expanding inside of her. "What?"

"If the one that means more to him than anyone else can forgive him." Scott lightly stroked her cheek. "I made assumptions I shouldn't have. I thought seeing me in the hospital brought up too many bad memories for you. In my profession, accidents can happen. I couldn't deal with the thought of putting you through seeing me that way again."

"If I couldn't have handled the risk, I never would have gotten involved with you."

"I know. I should have had more faith in you and not walked away. I'm sorry. But if you take me back,

I'll make up for it. I'm all in on doing whatever it takes for us to be together."

Rina closed her eyes, part of her wondering if she was imagining his words and his touch. She wanted to forgive him. But she'd let herself wrongly believe what Scott wanted before he'd left. If he was back at Tillbridge, he might just want a short-term thing, but she couldn't do that with him. She needed more. "What do you think we have?"

The warmth from his mouth hovered over hers as Scott spoke. "A shot at forever." He curved his hands around her waist. "I didn't always believe in it, but I do now."

Rina opened her eyes and looked directly into his. "Why?"

"Because I'm in love with you."

Telling him she felt the same was lost in Scott's kiss. Happiness welled inside of her along with the need to tell him everything. Her hopes. Her dreams. Her mistakes. Scott couldn't take all the blame. She pulled slightly away from him and rested her hands on his chest. "When you were in the hospital, I didn't come to you right away, because I was afraid of losing you. I should have been up front with you, too."

"I know you were scared. So was I. That's why I told myself that it was best to spare you from whatever you were feeling instead of giving you a chance to cope with it. But the truth is, when I saw the fear in your eyes, all I could see was you leaving me, if not then, sometime in the future. I was scared of losing you. Losing us."

Rina cupped his cheek. "I love you and I'm not going anywhere."

Tired of being ignored, Showdown gave a snort and a full body shake before turning away from them.

They both laughed.

Scott tipped his head toward Showdown. "He's yours by the way. I bought him for you."

"Thank you." Having Scott and Showdown back in her life was almost too much to absorb all at once. "I'm surprised you were able to convince Frank to part with him."

"The way you two have bonded, it was obvious where Showdown belonged. And I hope you're prepared to see me a lot more often. Kyle scoped out some land outside of Bolan. He's thinking about opening a stunt training school and wants me to join him in some capacity, an instructor, maybe even as a part owner. I said yes."

"If that makes you happy, but I'm not expecting you to give up your career for me. You have your passion and I have mine." He was about to become the first person to know what was on her business horizon. "My online store opens in five months. Pies for now, and later on, recipe kits and branded items."

Scott's grin widened as he picked her up in a hug. "I'm proud of you." He set her down and kissed her. "I'm going to love tempting people with your desserts. They're coming with me everywhere I go."

She liked the sound of that and having him around more. "I never thought I'd say this, but I'm so glad you ran me over and smashed my blueberry pies."

"Almost ran you over. And like I said. It was my greatest stunt ever."

"You're still sticking with that, huh?"

"Yep. And it will always be the greatest." His smile lit up the love in his eyes and touched her heart. "Because it gave me you."

* * * * *

Don't miss Zurie's story,
coming in February 2020
from Harlequin Special Edition!

And Tristan's story,

The Cowboy's Claim,

is available now wherever
Harlequin Special Edition
books and ebooks are sold.

WE HOPE YOU ENJOYED THIS BOOK FROM

HARLEQUIN

SPECIAL EDITION

Believe in love. Overcome obstacles. Find happiness.

Relate to finding comfort and strength in the support of loved ones and enjoy the journey no matter what life throws your way.

6 NEW BOOKS AVAILABLE EVERY MONTH!

COMING NEXT MONTH FROM

ⓗ HARLEQUIN

SPECIAL EDITION

Available October 27, 2020

#2797 HIS CHRISTMAS CINDERELLA
Montana Mavericks: What Happened to Beatrix?
by Christy Jeffries
Jordan Taylor has it all—except someone to share his life with. What he really wants for Christmas is to win the heart of Camilla Sanchez, the waitress he met at a charity ball. Camilla thinks they are too different to make it work, but Jordan is determined to prove her wrong—in three weeks!

#2798 SOMETHING ABOUT THE SEASON
Return to the Double C • by Allison Leigh
When wealthy investor Gage Stanton arrives at Rory McAdams's struggling guest ranch, she's suspicious. Is he just there to learn the ranching ropes or to get her to give up the property? But their holiday fling soon begins to feel like anything but—until Gage's shocking secret threatens to derail it.

#2799 THE LONG-AWAITED CHRISTMAS WISH
Dawson Family Ranch • by Melissa Senate
Maisey Clark, a struggling single mom, isn't going to suddenly start believing in Christmas magic. So what if Rex Dawson found her childhood letter to Santa and wants to give her and her daughter the best holiday ever? He's just passing through, and love is for suckers. If only his kisses didn't feel like the miracle she always hoped for...

#2800 MEET ME UNDER THE MISTLETOE
Match Made in Haven • by Brenda Harlen
Haylee Gilmore *always* made practical decisions—except for one unforgettable night with Trevor Blake! Now she's expecting his baby, and the corporate cowboy wants to do the right thing. But the long-distance mom-to-be refuses to marry for duty—she wants his heart.

#2801 A SHERIFF'S STAR
Home to Oak Hollow • by Makenna Lee
Oak Hollow, Texas, was supposed to be a temporary stop between Tess's old life in Boston and the new one in Houston. But when her daughter, Hannah, wraps handsome police chief Anson Curry—who also happens to be their landlord—around her little finger, Tess is tempted for the first time in a long time.

#2802 THEIR CHRISTMAS BABY CONTRACT
Blackberry Bay • by Shannon Stacey
With IVF completely out of her financial reach, Reyna Bishop is running out of time to have the child she so very much wants. Her deal with Brady Nash is purely practical: no emotion, no expectation, no ever-after. It's foolproof...till the time she spends with Brady and his warm, loving family leaves Reyna wanting more than a baby...

**YOU CAN FIND MORE INFORMATION ON UPCOMING HARLEQUIN TITLES,
FREE EXCERPTS AND MORE AT HARLEQUIN.COM.**

HSECNM1020

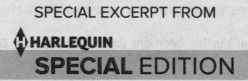
"Sweet dreams, little one," he said and stepped out of
the room.

She took off Hannah's shoes and jeans, then tucked
her in for the night. With a bolstering breath, she braced
herself for being alone with her fantasy man.

He stood in the center of the living room, looking
around like he'd never seen his own house. She
followed Anson's gaze to the built-in shelves she'd
filled with precious and painful memories. Things she
wasn't ready to share with him. Before he could ask any
questions, she opened the front door.

"Even though we were coerced, thank you for carrying her home. And for the house tour." Their "moment" in his bedroom flashed before her. *Damn, why'd I bring that up?*

"Anytime." Anson's blue-eyed gaze danced with amusement before he ducked his head and stepped outside. "Sleep well, Tess."

Fat chance of that.

She closed the door to prevent herself from watching him walk away. Tonight, Anson hadn't treated her indifferently like before and, in fact, seemed to be fighting his own temptations. Sometimes shutters would fall over his eyes as he distanced himself, then she'd blink and he'd wear his devil's grin, drawing her in with flirtation. Maybe he wasn't as immune to their attraction as she'd thought.

"I can't figure you out, Chief Anson Curry. But why am I even bothering?"

Don't miss
A Sheriff's Star *by Makenna Lee,*
available November 2020 wherever
Harlequin Special Edition books and ebooks are sold.

Harlequin.com